THE HOUR OF THE MILK
IS NO LONGER WHITE
A novella of philosophic transcendence

by Ronald Isaac Landau

i

Published by Landau & Associates.
PO Box 924
Cordova, TN 38018-0924 USA

ISBN# 1-881215-00-8   Library of Congress # 92-90089

I have made every effort to appropriately acknowledge all source material and to secure permission from copyright holders. In the event of any question arising as to the source of any material, I will be pleased to make the necessary acknowledgment in future printings.

Dedication

Ferdinand Landau
Reed B. Resneck
Dan Cocklin
Gabriel Ervin

Were there no ordering of the soul and of the state, no human society could survive; indeed, no civilized individual could endure[1]

Machiavelli puts the emphasis not on prophets but on armed prophets; among whom he counts Cyrus, Romulus, and Theseus, as well as Moses to unarmed prophets like Savonarola. He states the lesson which he intends to convey with remarkable candor: Armed prophets succeed and the unarmed ones come to ruin.[2]

I may be down but my eyes are open.

author unknown

Table of Contents

Part I
Robson

I left the synagogue this morning in disgust. If there are credentials for clergymen, in this day and age, life experience is surely not one of them.

Clergymen should be 60 or older and former men of action.

Let these men preach to us, bury our dead, marry our young, and console our sick for five years; then let someone like themselves take their place.

There should be no permanent clergy.

Liberal Northern clerics come into Southern synagogues with a culture and mind set I find not only foreign but unrealistic. There is an absence of hard work and hard living, and far too much Talmudic escapism or some other escapism.

I returned to Robson to feed my cattle.

I turned on the news, only to listen to personalized commentaries on the crumbs of news selected for me tonight.

Media clerics.

The excesses of freedom, when driven to a certain point, become Big Brother, or some other madness.

Electronic commercialism has crossed the line into insanity.

Hype. Hype. Hype. Imagery and propaganda everywhere and in everything; Americans are overstimulated and numb . . . a people unable to identify.

A nation of slaves.

The electronic media behave as though they were a substitute for thought. Not by informing, but by explicating do they illegitimatize themselves. Selective interviewing, empty-wagon stories, excessive creationism, and the attempt to make themselves the news, perpetrate falsehood. The attention of the electronic media is often about the base by the base.

Television has become but a chorus of sinister voices that together are coherent in their incoherence. When television is not used as an instrument to enhance the spirit and the mind, it becomes a weapon.

When they speak it is: "That's OK, and that's OK, and you shouldn't do that, but that's OK, and that's wrong, but I guess that's OK." Even many of the so-called "thinkers" are but Willy Lomans trying to make the sale for the manufacturer.

I watched the Israelis and the Arabs who live in Israel fighting on TV tonight.

The Jews are unsure of their own belongings.

A golden calf was built in the soul of Israel when Menachem Begin welcomed the Nazi-admiring Sadat into Israel as a guest.

The Egyptians understood very well the words of Sir Basil H. Liddell Hart when he said,

> *The object in war is to obtain a better peace even if only from your own point of view.*[3]

The diplomatic land-grab of the Sinai by the Egyptians was a masterstroke.

Mr. Begin's decision to turn over the Sinai to Egypt for an "Egyptian peace" was an act of treason against God and against Israel.

The Sinai is Israel, and the deed is registered in the book of Joshua.

Mr. Begin feared the United States and Egypt more than he feared God. Only the Jews are capable of allowing a vanquished enemy to dictate terms to them.

Perfidy.

During the negotiations for the transfer of Sinai from Israel to Egypt, General Ariel Sharon checked British surveying records for accuracy. In so doing, he behaved in accordance with the whims and by the whims of others. He chose not to seek command from his Bible, where his true dictums awaited him.

General Sharon then went on to destroy Yamit, a Jewish town in Sinai (Israel).

Would Napoleon have turned on Paris for the sake of making a peace with Prussia? I think not.

The Jew thrives on building bigger and bigger monuments to his defeated.

Mr. Begin, rest easy in your new residence. Your lapse shall be overturned as David's lapse was overturned.

The new Secretary General of the Ununited Nations is an Egyptian. The grand forces solidify to encircle. The growing, seemingly impenetrable circle of teeth composed of armed but fearful nations align as the declining embryo of the new one.

I remember watching on television the Israeli diplomat, Mr. Benjamin Netanyahu, tell the Arab press in Spain that he would be delighted to answer all their questions. He snapped to like a member of the Judenrat.

There is no more beautiful sight in the world than the rolling hills of East Tennessee. I would be content to live my eternity here. This is rural country, and I am a product of both its virtues and vices. I have a high school education and lifetime of work.

If the country and the media were run by some of the men in this county, the truth would not be such a scarce commodity.

I sat down on the porch and lit my Davidoff cigar. I smoke the Dominican Republic Davidoff's not the Cuban. I could acquire the Cubans but I don't.

Man's world is a was being pulled forward. We are but light travelling after the death of a star from a deeper present into a lesser present that is a deeper present. We are but a forward thinking afterthought deep in the midst of thought.

It's 4:30 a.m. and it feels like snow is on the horizon. I

love the bitter cold because it makes me feel alive.

The cattle seem almost self-aware this morning. The fear of death never enters their mind, but it's on my mind because I have bills to pay.

I had breakfast this morning at Barkay's as I've done for the last 30 years. The topic of conversation this morning was the anarchy in Los Angeles.

The nation may soon find itself broken off into at least autonomous city states.

Miscarriages.

Materialism.

Koreans returning home to Korea.

I received a message on my code-a-phone from June Prescott. I finished my lunch. Beef stew. I swallowed my Boilermaker, which I treat myself to on Friday afternoons, and went into town.

I've known June since we were children. Her father and my father were friends. Both farmed here when farming was all manual.

I walked into June's office and she gave me a big hug and a kiss. I felt warm all over. We talked until about 6:00 p.m. about life and love; and such, as we always have.

We were close in our early twenties, and I loved her deeply in a certain way. She married a fine man, and I'm very happy for her. I think we try to find time to spend together because we're soul mates. She's kept my poetry through the years as I have kept her smile and the sound of her laughter.

The residue of my visit with June is always the same; I come away feeling.

There are now 6 inches of snow on the ground and I've had a good day.

The shadow of illusion is becoming more and more clear to me. Henry P. Stapp said,

> *Everything we know about nature is in accord with the idea that the fundamental processes of nature lie outside space-time . . . but generate events that can be located in space-time.*[4]

Saturdays in winter I go to Archie McNatts, watch Tennessee football, and play chess. Archie's 74 and played football at Tennessee back in the 30's. We used to go up for games now and again, but Archie's had a couple of heart attacks and his daughter doesn't want him going up there anymore.

Archie was born in the Kentucky Appalachians with barely enough to eat growing up. He was the only one in his family to even graduate high school. He studied agriculture and history. He's the only man I've ever known who could make an analogy between pesticides and the Trojan War, in the same breath, and be right on both counts.

Tennessee lost to Alabama again this year, and I lost twice in chess. Archie's Indian defense is superb, and I've yet to break it. His daughter Carolyn had brisket for dinner. I ate and went home.

I couldn't sleep because I saw the United States replaced by another country, "New Africa."

Beside New Africa was Greater Mexico consisting of Southern California, New Mexico, Arizona, and south Texas.

The White Man is on his way to extinction and it is scaring the hell out of him.

Inheritance is a strange thing.

New separatist arrangements will provide a return home for many.

I am glad I won't live to see it.

The great mother of my civility is Europe. She whelped me, and I have grown in her image. Her dark sister is soon to overtake her. So does the consciousness of God expand. To this one, whelped by Europe, it expands against me.

Robson is all in church today but me. My mind is electric today focusing on everything and nothing. It happens when I'm lonely and take a lull in my reading.

I took a long walk this afternoon with my dog Dali; he's an Akita.

I call him Dali because he has a black streak running across his face that makes him oddly enough resemble the surrealist painter. Dali acquired his name this way.

I had always wanted an Akita after seeing one in Japan on my stopover to Korea, and hearing the story about an Akita, who for ten years, everyday returned to the train station to welcome home his master who had long since died.

We walked through the snow up to the Mac T's Auto Parts parking lot where I sat down, lit a cigar and for the moment felt at peace with the world.

I remembered some poetry of Yevgeny Yevtushenko, and thought.

> *There in Moscow in whirling darkness*
> *Wrapped in his military coat*
> *Not understanding Pasternak,*
> *A hard and cruel man stared at the snow.*[5]

I looked up at Dali and he was staring at me almost like a compassionate parent.

I walked by the First Baptist Church of Robson. It was close to dusk and quiet, me, Dali, and Josh ben Joseph upon the quiet snowy crossroad.

ben Joseph strived to live by the Law, as was prescribed by the God of Abraham, Issac and Jacob.

Minds are for the manifestation of the Law.

The Gentiles came between two feuding Jewish schools of thought.

The disciples were Jews writing a dissent. The disciples of Freud and Marx were no doubt of a similar vain. Gullible men racing to embrace the new false god.

The dissent is an over exuberant accounting of discord written by Utopians as a counter measure.

Never in the history of Man have words (the dissent) ever been so grossly misinterpreted while being so wrongly applied.

The dissent has behaved as a wild beast by transmission through the pagan and the heath-dweller who hold fast to the anger of the dissent while idolizing it and calling it Christianity.

The Gentiles have taken ben Joseph for themselves and made a god out of him while declaring themselves sin free only for the price of belief in this falsehood.

To hold such a position is blasphemy against creation because it negates the reason for the individual soul (as individual idea) in God's will.

Sin is negated by wisdom.

The Gentiles bow down to ben Joseph because they don't understand him.

To worship man as God is the pinnacle of ignorance, and is an attack upon God.

God is not a person but the principle of spirit, the spirit of principle.

ben Joseph the Jew has become a dagger in the hands of the Christians who use him as an excuse for their own crucifixions.

Alex Haley wrote,

> *If Christianity had asserted itself in Germany,*
> *six million Jews would have lived.*[6]

Mr. Haley doesn't see that Christianity did assert itself.

If the Christian cannot convert the Jew away from the Law, then the Christian must find a way to eradicate the

Jew along with his laws that bind him and threaten his existence in absurdity.

By fallacy alone do Christians attempt to tie Christianity to Judaism as a way of legitimizing Christianity.

The term Judeo-Christian is a false term. Judeo is the Orient, agrarians, and the worship of God, that has very often been the worship of self. Christian is Europe, hunters, and the worship of man, that has very often been the worship of killing men.

Frederick M. Schweitzer is a Roman Catholic who wrote in his book, *A History of the Jews Since the First Century A.D.,* the following:

> *In Vatican II's declaration, it is recalled that Jews and Catholics share the fatherhood of Abraham.*[7]

Abraham fathered two great nations: one through Ishmael (the Arabs), and one through Isaac (the Jews).

The Vatican's declaration of Christian lineage to Abraham is false and in more ways than one.

Christian writers have spent centuries trying to create themselves (Christians) a place within the Hebrew Bible; they have settled upon and for their illusionary bridges.

> *The great masses of the people will more easily fall victims to a big lie, than to a small one.*[8]
> — Adolf Hitler

The Christians claim that they are the wild branch grafted to the tree (Judaism). This is false. They are more truly a wild tree unable to stand naked before heaven alone.

Christianity aborts the Divine while at the same time it claims divine revelation.

Today Dogmatism in theology is so prevalent that true believers will do or say whatever is necessary to uphold anything at any cost.

I hold the belief that if there are realities in religion, they will be proclaimed by the convergence of mysticism and physics as experienced upon a plane where spiritual and material entities are not differentiated, but reflect unconditionally one autonomous idea.

Mysticism is the product of a fusion between imagination and intuition whose purpose is to further the will of heaven. From such a fusion, I can see the steam coming off the Ten Commandments.

Combine this with an applied physics that attempts to explain change, and what is left is probability.

The best probability for a human religion is a religion that will consent to trial and error.

The intended result is the rediscovery and reaffirmation of principle for the purpose of principle. Without this perspective as a foundation for a system of beginning human conduct, religion will remain a playground for weak-willed, undemonstrated thought.

Minds are for manifestation of the Law.

It would seem that mysticism and physics are conquered by the other as they conquer the other. A system of checks and balances is imperative in all religion, or it is a religion of fallacies.

The Brahmins believe that the goal of religion should be the illumination of consciousness.

Joseph would have made a wonderful Brahmin.

Joseph interpreted dreams while in an Egyptian prison. His capacity to do so was not because he was a focused empiricist, quite the contrary. His success was because he was a dreamer himself. He was an open gate for heaven. He was the sleeping butterfly in the musical current of nature. The language of symbolism was his language. Joseph's capacity to interpret could be compared to that of a theoretical mathematician. The ballet of intuition and symbolism not only predicts the future, but institutes and constitutionalizes it.

I dreamt that my essence was submerged in acid, the very same acid that was used to ignite the Big Bang of Creation. The acid recreates me. The acid laughed at me confident in its knowledge of creation. I run to my mother Europe to diffuse the designs of the acid as I dismiss its confident Negro laughter.

Monday was bitter cold also. I read in the paper where the Supreme Court said burning the flag is A-OK. I find nothing supreme in this decision.

The first load of my cattle was shipped to Kansas City this morning. There was one steer I thought rather odd and personable. He was scheduled to go this morning but I didn't have the heart. I'll call him Plato. When I decided to let him graze here for life, I was struck by the music on the radio. A choir from a monastery in Sicily singing Latin hymns. I am left off balance by the depth that the Gregorian Chant penetrates me. Its purity and beauty make my deepest hungry doors open with the grace of a grateful, freed servant.

I gazed out into the field at Plato. If I could do for the universe what I did for Plato, I would.

The movement of history is a violent drama most often played out by spoiled children. Ethics in the individual, immersed together and combined with the ethics of others, culminate in what Hegel would call the spirit of history. It is the culmination of noble and free thinking individuals that gives rise to periods like the Renaissance. Conversely, it is the many closed-minded that create eras like the Dark Ages and Communism. Wars, more often than not, are fought for the trinket-lovers under the guise of protecting culture.

Culture is the relationship between a man's heart and heaven.

Today, there is an uneasiness about the unethical practically everywhere. Thomas R. Malthus' theorems on the relation between population growth and the finitude of resources crystallizes as a dark shadow that hovers over as the essence of our age whose signature is starvation.

In the United States today, there are less and less farmers producing more and more food. The American farmer is creative and imaginative in his pursuits of efficiency. Agricultural efficiency and other forms of efficiency could be taught to and fro were it not for the selfish interests that block the exchanges in diversity of thought and opinion by the insatiable appetites of the unethical in search of their excesses. So does this age move many into the crypt.

George Bush is a man misfortunate enough to have to govern at a time when the racial makeup of the United States and the rest of the earth is moving rapidly from a first to a third world populace.

The posture of the declining European is of one fighting in retreat against the advancing man of the third world.

The European and his culture based on a reason of conquest has stylized for at least the last thousand years a sea of magnanamous and not so magnanamous ideas that in many ways render the present on all continents his own. The rigidity of European reason that for so long rendered its analytical splendor so beautifully in the heart of the European will also serve as his unwilling executioner, trapped in its rigidity by the onslaught of the third world multitudes and their contradictions.

George Bush's "New World Order" gives the appearance of a noble intent by the first world to try and work with the third world under the auspices of standards and principles. The Gulf War was such an example. It was a temporary phenomenon by two separate worlds that have designs on each other. Sacrifices will be needed to keep the peace between the two worlds that long to devour each other.

President Jimmy Carter sold out the Jews at Camp David thus making of Israel a sacrificial lamb by the first world sacrificed into the belly of the third world, as a means of temporary appeasement. Jimmy Carter was a modern Pontius Pilate, who sacrificed the Jews at Camp David, while believing himself a peacemaker. President Bush must be careful not to follow in the same manner as the ill-spirited Carter who could not endure the calamities that followed, and who was voted out of office by a citizenry with the taste of shame for the President in their mouths.

George Bush's "New World Order" in the end will come to represent a world alignment against Israel. An intended sacrifice from East to West and from West to East.

There was recently a Nazi running for the governorship of Louisiana. He received 55 percent of the White vote. The excuse-hungry seek to fill themselves in spite of their truths. The Whites will migrate from the Blacks and others of their own accord.

Judge Clarence Thomas spoke for four or five days in the confirmation process, and didn't speak his mind once. Robert Gates, a few days later, went before members of the Senate, and had no idea of anything concerning Iran-Contra, while flocks of men above and below him were operating like chickens with their heads cut off. It's disingenuous to ask the American people to promote men that stand before us under oath whose concentration of conscience is the perpetration of oblivion.

Compare Thomas' and Gates' testimony to that of Dmitry's in Fedor Dostoyevsky's *The Brothers Karamozov*. Language never outranks conscience.

The Nazi did respectively well because the electorate is fed up with the articulate nothingness of diplomatic language that is intended to inspire their consciences, but doesn't come from consciences.

There are men no matter what their political-philosophic perspective who blame. Their finger pointing at everything can't help but be right on occasion. Like spoiled angry children who have not gotten their way, they point and scream at the world as though they believe that they are the world. It is they who need spanking. They seek to engage and anger us. They seek to turn us on ourselves, as they feel intolerant toward responsibility while they speak of responsibility. They make love with themselves through the emptiness of their own words in front of us, while they expect us to stand and applaud. They look us in the eyes and say,

> *We are not responsible for your anger and meanness toward each other, nay, for we are here to make the peace between you - we are your peacemakers.*

The ascending human spirit finds itself where moral discipline meets difficult times.

American economists often speak of the American economy as a service-oriented economy. What they really mean, but are afraid to say, is that America has become the shoe-shine boy for the Orientals and the Europeans.

The American manufacturing base is collapsing, and America's weak trading position is ruthlessly being out-hustled. The rapid demise of society is due in large part to the many who espouse and manifest a La Cosa Nostra philosophy: the intent is always to shut out the freeman.

White-collar men, who would normally be managing and manufacturing, have become lawyers and PhD's, who now roam this country like lost souls looking for problems to solve, while blue-collar workers are angry and unsure who to blame.

Of all the citizens in the world, I believe the American to be the most forgiving and fair-minded of them all. However, many Americans have been sold out by other Americans who are highly invested in the Orient and by the U.S. government that overtaxes. The government does not pay its bills, yet feels free to burden the backs of our children's children with debt.

The government has become a racket where disorder has come to reign.

There is no honest disagreement but only the appearance of honest disagreement by those who pride themselves on openness while they cling to the status quo where they have a place.

There is too much fat. Money is created in real work, not in make work.

It will only be a matter of time before treasury bills become worthless, and the government collapses. Japan is growing weary from holding the United States up while Japan knocks the United States down.

Revolt is inevitable. Revolt with your minds and without hatred. Revolt with an angelic spirit for the angelic spirit.

Thomas Jefferson said something to the effect that the ability of the people to overthrow the government is the cornerstone of democracy.

The next American revolutionary war, if Americans are strong enough to fight it, shall be a war for personal independence. It shall be a war to recapture the mind.

The words of Carl Rogers (the humanistic psychologist) are apt:

> *We can choose to use our growing knowledge to enslave people in ways never dreamed of before, depersonalizing them, controlling them by means so carefully selected that they will perhaps never be aware of their loss of personhood.*[9]

Vance Packard wrote, in the *People Shapers,* about the three D's of conversion under coercion:

Debilitation, Dread, and Dependency,

All implemented in process upon the individual to bring him to the point of submission:

> *the prisoner is given a glimpse that his captors can be welcome friends if only he accepts their viewpoint.*[10]

This is a time hostile to the orphan, and the thoughts that only orphans can think.

Public libraries that could serve as a savior are empty, because the people know not why the libraries are there. Americans have become slaves. Humanity that doesn't think is destined for slavery.

The drug problem in America doesn't just entail drugs, but all unnecessary a-spiritual stimuli as well.

Food, for example, is with many an obsession. When I think of cane sugar, I think of Cain.

Hollow.

Cain wasn't able.

When empty stimuli bombard spirit, humans become idol worshippers and thus become idle.

A diet of raw fruits and vegetables would return many minds to their owners and with a much enhanced fuel tank.

Sex is another drug, if not blessed by love.

Did heaven not provide birth control to appease them? Are they not but slaves to their bodies? They scream concerning false rights at the expense of their own blood soul because they cannot make human beings out of themselves. Because they have cared not to prevent, it shall be they who are aborted; then prevented.

Aids.

Recently George Bush collapsed while meeting in Tokyo with the Japanese on trade. Trade to the Japanese is war. I have learned to have great respect for their discipline and ferocity. Their strength is strengthened by their knowledge that the United States is dying from within from decadence. The United States is no longer a sleeping giant but a diseased, slumbering drunk.

Whether his conscious mind knew it or not, George Bush stood before his new masters with his defeated captains by his side, petitioning for mercy. The proud nobility of George Bush's line placed in the position of having to render an unconditional surrender brought George Bush tumbling down to the feet of America's new masters.

The first time George Bush was shot down by the Japanese he could get up.

The principle of divide and conquer is systematically being perpetrated upon the American citizen by the socialist policies of the American government, by Japan, by the emptiness of television, from the pulpit, from the courts, and even from our next door neighbors who sue us for nothing. Forces from everywhere seek to divide us from ourselves, from each other, from our Constitution, and from our duty to principle.

On the day in 1948 when the UN declared the birth of the state of Israel, I was sitting on my porch. I remember looking up into the clouds and saw to my left both Mecca and the Vatican. I turned away for a moment, then looked up toward the two cities again only to see huge armies of salt statues.

Tuesday's mail held a surprise for me. I received an invitation to a cattle auction in Blackstone. I have been looking to buy some longhorn cattle, and now I have my chance.

The auction is in two weeks, and it will give me something to look forward to.

Ilysa sent me a letter today. Ilysa is old and alone like me. The difference between us is that she needs people and I don't. She stays active as a way of finding self-worth in her life.

I agree with Voltaire in that,

The happiest of all lives is a busy solitude.[11]

Ilysa has the carriage and grace of a queen.

Born in Germany, she escaped the Third Reich by leaving Germany in 1936. She arrived in the United States the same year. I met Ilysa about ten years ago at the symphony in Nashville.

We talked until dawn that evening and have become like brother and sister.

Ilysa invited me to hear a speaker tonight and I shall go with her.

The man speaking tonight is a Jewish professor who is going to speak about the Holocaust. He explained the fate of the Jews as the result of a moral void in the world and other externalities. Externalities are often those ideas that attempt to place the blame outside of the individual and his decision-making capacities in order to shirk responsibility.

In Elie Wiesel's *Night*, Wiesel refused to believe Moche who tried to warn everyone of their impending doom. Wiesel, in not listening to this warning, turned his back on God. It was not the case of God not listening to the Jews, but of the Jews not listening to God.

Isaiah 65:11,12

But ye that forsake the Lord,
That forget my holy mountain,
That prepare a table for fortune,
And that offer mingled wine in full measure unto destiny,
I will destine you to the sword.
And ye shall all bow down to the slaughter;
Because when I called, ye did not answer,
When I spoke, ye did not hear;

The Jews idolized the Law instead of obeying it.

If the Jews had been obeying the Law, they would have seen events as they were, and not as they wanted them to be.

The Law when properly applied is a medium to vision.

To ignore is to perpetrate the self-righteous suicide.

Meir Kahane's murderer was defended successfully by a Jew. It is rumored that this same Jewish lawyer may defend the Arabs that recently blew up the airplane over Scotland.

To defend the murderers of one's own people is treason.

It is the Jewish liberals who are always ready to point the finger and accuse others of anti-Semitism, while they defend terrorists and call it justice.

The American Jewish liberals fought Richard Nixon tooth and nail, but it was Nixon who put it on the line for the Jews during the 1973 Yom Kippur War.

From Ariel Sharon's book, *Warrior*, comes the following quote:

> *It is not widely known that since the Six-Day War Arabs from all over the Middle East have come to Israel for medical treatment. They have come from Saudi Arabia, from Iraq, from the Persian Gulf Emirates, from Egypt, from Jordan, even from Libya. Women who for years could not conceive have had their problems resolved here (Israel).* [12]

Healing one's mortal enemies is an affront to God. Such stands that contradict the Law will come back to haunt with a vengeance.

The liberal Jews are the world's foremost proponents of the false god of pseudo-humanism.

Israel conquers by settlements because it lacks the audacity, the will, and the faith to expel its enemies from its land.

The mistakes of antiquity all over again.

Israel appears as wounded prey on this matter and on other matters, because there exists no Jewish Right.

The Jews that turned on Meir Kahane shall neither be mourned nor remembered.

Rest easy old priest, thy will be done.

Moses was raised as an Aristocratic Egyptian, Spinoza wrote his best works as an ex-communicated exile on the outskirts of Amsterdam, and Herzl was an emancipated journalist. The world is more often than not moved forward by outsiders.

The Jew has serviced every nation and I am baffled by the price and waste of it all. The nations considered the service of the Jews as a dis-service.

The price of the veils.

The drive from Nashville to Robson is about 80 miles. Driving the back roads at night is like trying to think through the dark, vaguely seeable corridors of my mind.

I was glad to see Dali, as I pulled into the driveway. He always gives me a loving and austere welcome. The fire had gone out in the fireplace, so I used the professor's lecture brochure to restart it.

The weather broke this morning; it's supposed to get up to 23° today. The winds of summer are blowing my way.

I picked up some corn feed this morning and it's more expensive than last year.

I have a couple of sick cattle, and Doc Thomas won't make it out until tomorrow. Rural vets are the aristocracy in my world and R.J. Thomas especially. I would love to attain an oral history of civilization starting with the first veterinarian back in the fertile crescent downwards and up to Doctor Rudolf Josepé Tomiliano (Doc Thomas).

I watched Firing Line tonight. William F. Buckley spoke on the Cold War and the political and social movement in the East.

Lies, be they in the East under Communism or in the West under Capitalism, are the same moral dysfunction that will always come to be purged in the end.

White Russia will begin to feel isolated in its newly acquired freedoms, vulnerable, like the Israel of the North, but without a tradition in the sincere application of laws. Russia shall find itself surrounded by hostile former republics with long memories and heavy weapons, as well as the metastasizing of Islamic fundamentalism.

Until China awakens, the cross in Russia will seek to keep at bay the crescent (true everywhere now) as many Jews of Russia return to Israel.

The Jew is the lubricant between different peoples because of his dreamy idealism. The Jews sudden absence in Russia leaves the different hard peoples anxious.

The United States is now free to collapse, now that the Soviet Union has collapsed. They were as two legs pressing against each other in order to stand. For far too

long each escaped into the refuge of the other at the
expense of themselves.

This morning I'm taking my truck to Reginald Pierce's.
He's the only diesel mechanic in Robson, and one of the
only Blacks. He was raised here then moved to Philadel-
phia when he was twelve, found himself in Vietnam at
17, and almost buried at 18.

We had lunch after he worked on my truck, and we
swapped stories as we always do. I admire Reggie, not so
much because he took a degree in engineering and I
never went to college, but because he's as honest as the
day is long.

I go to Reggie's for dinner on occasion and his kids call
me the Bad Wolf because I raise so much hell with them.
I rejoice in the spontaneity and exuberance of children;
they are life sustaining.

I don't know what process in life makes some men lose
this. Wordsworth attempted to tell those of us who are
grown that we must try and recapture the innocence of
our childhood.

Recently I went into court and was advised by the
judge not to appear without an attorney, and that no
matter how well prepared I was, the judgement from the
bench would go against me. This came to pass in spite of
the fact that the facts in my case were overwhelmingly in
my favor.

The law is inaccessible to those it is intended to protect,
because the courts feel that out of expediency paid

interpreters (lawyers) must be present.

I find lawyers to interpret mostly among themselves and for themselves.

The law has become a business where the inflection of rhetoric and procedure by third parties (lawyers) is determined to keep disagreements between men a tradeable commodity.

Men must be able to speak for themselves to each other without interference, or the law will not function in the spirit that it was intended.

I appealed my case, hired an attorney, and won my case.

Courts are arenas where synthetic gladiators fight with synthetic weapons (words) that kill and destroy others but not themselves.

This is a dishonest time, where many men shirk facing one another to boil out truths. Truths are not their motives. Honest men feel an aversion at having to go to court. Deceits have infiltrated even unto the men of the distant fields. Those who have been entrusted to keep are the ones that have positioned themselves to steal while appearing lawful. They believe that no one sees them as they laugh amongst themselves.

I was happy to get my truck repaired. I have always been concerned about the health of things around me. Animate or not, I feel that I have personal relationships with the things in my world.

The snow has melted down somewhat in the last

couple of days, and driving is better. I like driving in snow
and ice from time to time. My old age and the hazardous
conditions make my mind wake up, as it propels my eye-
hand coordination to the limit.

I only wish I could be induced to raise my skill level with
the ladies in the same way. Rarely does a woman's
sexuality present itself to me in the same manner as an
ice slick road with a 180° gradient. The only sex I get
nowadays is a shave in Barney's barbershop.

I watched a group of ants devouring a sugar cube on my
kitchen floor. Then I thought how the Amazon rain forest
is being destroyed, how the elephants in Africa are being
killed for their tusks, and about the dolphins being killed
by the millions because of indifferent and mean-spirited
fishermen.

Japan's waste management policy is the most sound in
the world. Japan is a nation that plunders others' trees
but not their own. Japan is a blessed nation of structure
solely in need of the ways of artists. The embrace of
nature shall free many from ghosts.

All in their own way.

Japan dreams of Chinese markets, while China con-
templates Japan's most recent atrocities upon them.

China will outsmart Japan.

The earth is being plundered by a species of remorse-
less tomb robbers.

Plants and animals have souls that, if not respected,
will come to punish the disrespectful by absence.

The Cogi Indians of Columbia believe themselves to be the guardians of the heart, of the Great Mother, and I believe them. They warn that the mountains have become dry because the clouds have been stolen. The rivers born in the mountains are no longer being born, so the waters below are drying up and not administering life.

The whole human lot sleeps in the thoughts of the coolness of their past, not feeling the incremental boil that shall soon consume them.

We have made the oceans untouchable, where they are no longer our lifeline, but our death line.

Does not a thing flow back unto itself?

Even the residue of madness must find its proper channel.

There are nights that I can't sleep because I hear the cries of my own cattle that I have sent to slaughter.

The lion lying down with the lamb is Man returning to a vegetarian existence.

Whether the earth shall resign itself before Man can make this transformation will be realized soon.

I sat down in front of the fireplace and tried to empty my mind. I want a vacation from the production. I just want to be the proof of seeds as trees as seeds.

I baked a potato and cooked a filet for dinner. I fed Dali then ate my own dinner. He always stares me down for my dinner. I kind of like it, because I feel as if I am not eating alone, and that my company's mind is not wandering off; quite the contrary.

We began our after dinner walk. I always walk down to Points Bluff. It runs through the back side of a state park and all my neighbors usually walk the same route, so a lot of evenings it's a social call. Tonight it was just Dali and me.

I heard on the news today that some of the Chinese students who marched in Tiennamen Square were executed.

I remember watching the events from the beginning. The students' uprising was civil in nature and was carried out in the manner of celebration. It was a beautiful thing to watch, the young Chinese experiencing the necessary ideals of their minds.

Unlike Russia, China will move slowly and carefully into democracy. China is harmony conscious, not rash.

I had similar feelings about the Black Civil Rights movement in the 1960's.

The true civil rights of the Black man will not come from the Constitution of the United States but from the Constitution of heaven.

He will impose by the strength of his own will a Carthaginian peace, upon the remnants of the slave masters.

Martin King was obsessed with the external and not the internal. Had he sought to advance upon the internal, the many would have followed instead of divided.

Pseudo-legal trinkets from Egypt are no substitute for

the mystical freedoms found in the Law.

The Blacks are dying from a lack of introspection.

There shall be peace for them when the house Negroes re-enter the soul of the community of field Negroes, unless they destroy themselves first.

Today they terrorize themselves through self enslavement.

Many a Black procreates without discrimination or for discrimination.

The American Black community destroys itself while it sings "We Shall Overcome."

To the rest they are illegitimate when they speak and march concerning morals, as they kill themselves in droves. Their self destruction is draining away vital energy that, instead of sustaining civilization, is depleting civilization. They are a people obsessed with the veneer. They long for governmental socialism because they have no inner socialism.

They will not overcome, but shall inherit.

Africa, at last!

The Whites enslaved the Blacks with chains in the last century. The Blacks will enslave the Whites in the next century by drowning them in a sea of incoherence. The structured drowned in structurelessness.

Many of the Black schools are an extension of the flourishing, undisciplined wounded that are the Black community as a whole.

The Black elders are not firm with their young, because

the elders are not in themselves possessed of firmness.

The Blacks are unable to reach themselves. The numbers of the Black unreached outweighs the numbers of the Black reached. The reached will not have the strength to carry their unreached brethren when soon they shall be all alone together.

The Black's habitual knee-jerk response to everything as racist is often an irresponsible weapon in the hands of the irresponsible in order to excuse the inexcusable. It is often a substitute for focus.

Black on Black crime is a racism that the Blacks disregard. This is shameful, but the Blacks feel no shame because of it. There is no honor in suicide and denial.

Their guilt is the mark of their pride and of their manhood.

The Blacks are not the only ones who have turned on themselves in this century; Europeans, Russians, Chinese, Arabs, and Cambodians all reel from recent self-inflicted wounds.

The result of closed systems.

Judaism and the Law will be where many Blacks find refuge.

Slavery cannot mother coherence.

The Israelites wandered in the desert for forty years after receiving the Law. The desert was less barren than the thought patterns in the minds of the newly freed Hebrew slaves.

Jews of today often behave as over-educated slaves.

Such behavior had a hand in the Holocaust.

Dali and I walked up past Tennyson's lumber mill. The smell up here is wonderful. Tennyson is a smart man because he replants from what he takes. Replanting keeps the view from the bluff beautiful, as the little green trees all grouped together below look like playing children.

Hobbies Lake is a couple of miles from the bluff, and I fish there in the summer. I like to eat sunfish and trout, while everything else is given away.

Dali and I got in at 8:00 p.m. and I watched a glorious movie tonight on TV, entitled "Brazil." The film was a futuristic commentary concerning the freedom to think. It is a striking parody of our own times.

The threat to internally free men comes from internally unfree men.

Some will walk toward the caves now, in the hope of saving those left who may have to run toward the caves later.

Alexander and Napoleon conquered by the force of arms; Lenin and the Communists by ideology; the next conqueror will do so by the control of commodities while claiming that men's minds, spirits and thoughts are free.

I bought some Trump Taj Mahal first mortgage bonds. Trump's a pretty boy in vogue, who in spite of the fact that he is headed for financial disaster can't depreciate real estate but so much. Trump thought he could own the world on borrowed money, as did Robert Maxwell.

Hubris.

My sick cattle are looking much better. The price of beef went up sharply this month, I guess I may get those new shower curtains after all. I saw Plato chasing Dali in the pasture. I love a pronounced and playful individualism in anything.

Dr. Zhivago is on TV tonight. My chance to understand Pasternak has arrived. I've waited all week to watch it. It elicits in me a romantic Russian strain that seems to plug my mind into a different circuit, if only for a few hours. I left a message on June's machine to watch it. I'm the only one who calls her about such things.

Watching Dr. Zhivago was grand. Zhivago was a poet and physician, a healer of the spirit and the body. I admire Zhivago because he fought to maintain himself as a gentleman in the midst of a crumbling civilization.

Zhiv means *to live* in Russian.

I lay down on my bed and thought of my mother's father. He was a Karaite from Sebastopol on the Crimean peninsula. When I was very young he would come and visit us. He had long grey hair to the middle of his back and a long grey beard. His mind was formed by the forces of the Hebrew Bible, Russian poetry, and vodka. He had even dabbled with his Muslim neighbors on the virtues of Sufism. He was a man both in and out of this world.

I awoke, looked out my window and saw Robson. It's good to be back. Tomorrow. Tennessee plays Kentucky at Neyland Stadium, and it's supposed to snow.

I remember seeing flies on the faces of the children of

Bombay and the children were not even cognizant of them. Yet, I watched Dali become incensed that even one fly would attempt to land on him. I have raised my dog as a human being, and he conducts himself as such. It is odd to watch India's children starve as their animals feast.

India's kindness towards creation is sound, but without a procurement for their children, it is incomplete.

India cannot lead until it strikes the balance.

Tomorrow I will go to Archie's to watch Tennessee vs. Kentucky. Today college football is white generals and black tribes.

College football to the Southerner is in many ways a symbolic continuation of the Civil War. The rebel flag is visible in Oxford, Mississippi today as it was 130 years ago. Southerners in the right or in the wrong were and are an honor-conscious people. The Southerner's genuine instinctual sense of honor found itself shamed, when compared with the greater truths of higher laws found within a Union victory.

As I look at a quiet Archie, I see a great but hurt dignity of a man and of a people who often rejoice and weep louder than the rest on Saturday afternoons.

Archie is a most righteous man. King David came from the line of Ruth, a convert, and he was, except for Moses, our greatest fighting son. Righteous gentiles make superb Jews. In the end, they shall have no other option but darkness. We are as far away as they, but from another direction.

Of the intermarriages between Jews and Gentiles, the Jews may add two percent while losing the rest.

I stayed until about 10:00 p.m.. Archie and I discussed *The Ascent of Man* by Jacob Bronowski.

Agriculture is the key to civilization.

Today in the United States, the insurance companies are quietly buying up as much farm land as they can get their hands on in order to assure themselves a power base over those freedoms that insure civilization.

The future is more than ever food and water.

I was told once by an Englishman that in his country, everyone has a small plot or garden. This would seem to be the best defense against a global monopolization of the food industry. A personal relationship with the earth does wonders for the spirit of the soul.

I got into bed about midnight. I dreamt that someone was coming towards me. As he came closer, I began to hear traditional Japanese music. The music presented itself as an oxymoron. It was a persona of delicacy belied by enormous natural force. It seemed to name itself to me as "Thunder in Springtime." The man looked to be and was an old warlord. He walked right through me. As he entered me as an abode of spirit, I can now hear the laughter of the birds and trees.

In waking, I am fixed in contemplation that is travelling upon a beam of light from my unconscious state to my conscious state. It would seem that Einstein's theory of relativity is wrong because to God, everything is relative and nothing is relative.

I took a long drive with Dali today to look at a piece of land I was thinking of buying. It didn't appear to me as its owner described it over the phone. Man plans and God laughs. It's when man begins to laugh with God that he begins to find himself.

I'm glad to be home. When I enter my home the purple dancing Chagall on my wall always welcomes me. Tonight, again I hear the Japanese instrumental Thunder in Springtime.

I cooked some pre-packaged beef Stroganoff for dinner. I could have used it to lay brick; instead I ate it because I was hungry. I gave some to Dali, but he wouldn't eat it; he preferred his Alpo. Tonight I think I'll stare him down for his dinner.

The market was up again today. I think it's overpriced.

My father lost everything in the crash.

He sold apples, cut grass, washed windows, did what had to be done.

My father was a German educated in the classics and in the art of war. It broke my heart as a small child to watch him in such a humble state. He sat me down one evening and told me how his parents were peasants and not to be ashamed of his low station. It's not what a man does, but the way he does it that should make him proud or shameful, and as a result, I have tried to live my life as a proud laborer.

Reflecting on my father's predicament brings to mind

a thought in a book I read years ago in Paul Tillich's *The Courage To Be.*

I think a man can attain the courage to be only when he is turned back at every attempt to escape. Only when cornered like a rat and desperate beyond his capacity will he collapse into his own arms to be pulled into the highest of freedoms.

Tonight, on TV, I watched a Black preacher pleading with his audience, "Keep hope alive." I had seen this preacher before, and others like him. In Friedrich Nietzsche's *Thus Spoke Zarathustra:*

> *The preachers of equality, the tyrannomania of impotence clamors thus out of you for equality: your most secret ambitions to be tyrants thus shroud themselves in words of virtue.*
> *Aggrieved conceit, repressed envy, perhaps the conceit and envy of your fathers—erupt from you as a flame and as the frenzy of revenge.*
> *When they become elegant and cold, it is not the spirit but envy that makes them elegant and cold. Their jealousy leads them even on the paths of thinkers: out of every one of their complaints sounds revenge; in their praise there is always a sting, and to be a judge seems bliss to them.*
> *They are people of low sort and stock; the hangman and the bloodhound look out of their faces.*
> *Not around the inventors of new noise but around*

the inventors of new values does the world revolve.
It revolves inaudibly.
Admit it!
Whenever your noise and smoke were gone,
very little had happened.[13]

Existence feels like transcendence within transcendence. I often feel like I am being spun upon a spinning floor.

I am having difficulty distinguishing my day-to-day living from dreams, as dreams within dreams.

I'm going to the supermarket today. I need just about everything. Dali loves cheese slices and milk bones, both of which are at the top of my list. He's supposed to stud a female in 2 months, and I can already see he's got the itch.

I bumped into Annie Williams at the market today. Her husband is Billy Williams, Pastor Billy Williams. Billy's father was a pastor, too. I like Billy, but he tends to shy away from me. I don't hold it against him. One thing I'll give Billy, he knows his Bible, and he tries to live by it.

Billy was the first to welcome me home from Korea, but I didn't know this until 10 years after the fact. At the time I was bandaged up pretty good, and was on enough morphine to make an elephant do stand-up comedy. Shortly after the war I had written an article in a philosophy journal concerning Christianity. The historians and logicians found it thought-provoking, but the Christian clerics called it "blasphemy of the highest order." Billy read my article and has been distant from me ever since, and we grew up together. I was hurt by this, but I learned something from it.

The Christian fears the Jew in his heart of hearts because the Jew is a living testament to the invalidity of Christianity.

The Jews, a tiny numerical people within the grand scheme, are also feared because they are the fundamental changemakers of the fundamental. Abraham, Moses, Freud, Marx and Einstein are but a few examples that have forced the many inflexible fearful into the face of the new fundamental mirrors.

I talked with Annie in the market for a little while. She said Billy still brings my name up on occasion. We parted ways and I was confirmed in my hunch that Billy still had a warm spot in his heart for me as I do for him.

I read where more and more Black people in America are throwing off Christianity and becoming Moslems.

If I were a Black man I wouldn't put my eternal faith in the White man's faith either.

However, the transition into Islam can also be where angels fear to tread. The outer display of discipline and conservatism by Islam is belied by an outlook and readiness for extremism and martyrdom. If martyrdom were in God's repertoire God would have had Abraham execute Isaac.

Martyrdom for the sake of martyrdom is an affront to God.

This dark Eastern way has also long danced without restraint and with delight inside Christianity. Behind curtains without conscience they are named cathedrals and mosques of God and worship. I see these twins darken each others' darkness.

The Black man must find his own god in his own way if he is to save himself.

Tomorrow I am going to a cattle auction.

The last longhorn I had killed a mule. I hope the ones I buy tomorrow are less cantankerous.

I like auctions. I mostly go to see old friends and talk shop.

Farmers in general are having a tough time, more men trying to sell more cattle than ever.

The small farmer is being squeezed out of the markets by multi-national corporations and coalitions of corporations. Whether the spirit of the American marketplace is laissez faire or unfair I don't know. I do know that two cattlemen and a soybean farmer, all of whom I knew, have committed suicide all within six months of each other. Cayton Owen, Bobby Culpepper, and Jason C. Stratems were all driven to their deaths by the marketplace.

Japanese holdings in the U.S. may be expropriated.

The auction was a disappointment, although I did buy a beautiful quarter horse. I'll call him Shorty. He rode well this afternoon — he'll make a great companion. He, Dali, Plato, Ralph my rooster, all my other cattle and a few goats keep me feeling like old Noah. The only animals I never got to raise were children. I'll carry this disappointment inside me for the duration.

There will be a vast resettlement of White people in the West in the next century. Montana, Alaska, Idaho, Wyoming, and the Dakotas among others will find themselves as the haven states for the White flight.

As the Blacks become the majority in big cities, the picture of East St. Louis today will be the norm of the Black-run city tomorrow.

I believe the capital of the United States will eventually be moved out west.

I enjoy going to bed at night. A friend once said to me, Karl, you're sleeping your life away. I thought for a moment and said, "There are worse ways to live this life. Besides, I don't have a dream debit like the rest of you."

Today was a long day.

Dali is sleeping on the sofa in front of the fireplace; he's such a peaceful creature.

I have a copy of the Chandogyu Upanisad on my night table, although I think I'll wait and start it tomorrow.

I began to see more clearly today a world of symbols, but yet, I could still differentiate all too clearly between spirit and materialism.

Like spoiled children, my analytical and transcendental capacities are fighting far too much in my being for there to be much progress; I'll work on it.

This morning I picked up parts to rebuild the carburetor

on my tractor. It should take me half a day to cure the patient. My fat, clumsy fingers, coupled with a weak mechanical aptitude and a wandering mind, will keep me in the belly of this tractor all day.

The patient should live to be a hundred.

I was up to my elbows in grease when the phone rang. It was Arnold Chattsworth.

He's an old friend and neighbor. He called to tell me that his first grandson was born and they were having a party tomorrow night. I told him thanks, and that I looked forward to it.

I showered, ate, and thought about Arnold's grandson. I then began to think about my father. He was a German who rarely spoke any English. He was a major in the German army during the First World War, and was wounded at the battle of Belleau Woods. The army discharged him because of the severity of his wounds.

He was a man pushing middle age, without a career. The loss of the war left him alone and at odds with the Fatherland, so he came to America to visit, but he stayed.

He once told me that the hills and forests of East Tennessee looked very much like the small town that he grew up in next to the Black Forest.

He met my mother in New York at an off-Broadway play, in which she was performing.

She came from Heidelberg in 1918 to pursue an acting career. She was the daughter of a Karaite cleric who had moved to Germany from Sebastopol at the turn of the century. I am a product of two races.

My parents were married in 1923 and I was born in 1929. Father died when I was 13 and mother when I was 16.

I recently came across the poem "Build Me a Son" by General Douglas McArthur.   Tomorrow when I go to Arnold's I will take a copy of the poem with me to give to his grandson. After reading it I Xeroxed a few copies, one of which I taped to the headstone over my father's grave.

Build me a son, O Lord,
Who will be strong enough to
Know when he is weak, and brave
Enough to face himself when he is
Afraid; one who will be proud
And unbending in honest defeat,
And humble and gentle in victory.
Build me a son whose wishes
Will not take the place of deed;
A son who will know thee
And that to know himself is the
Foundation stone of knowledge.
Lead him, I pray, not in the path
Of ease and comfort,
But under the stress and spur of difficulties and challenge,
Here let him learn to stand up
In the storm; here let him
Learn compassion for those who fail.
Build me a son whose heart will
Be clear, whose goal will be high,

A son who will master himself
Before he seeks to master other men,
One who will reach into the future
And never forget the past and
After all these things are his,
Add I pray, enough of a sense
Of humor, so that he may always
Be serious, yet never take himself too
Seriously. Give him humility, so that
He may always remember the simplicity
Of true greatness, the open mind
Of true wisdom, and the meekness of
True strength.
Then I, his father,
Will dare to whisper
I have not lived in vain.[14]

The birth of a child is always a blessing, because it brings one more comedian into the world, and the world is always in need of new and funnier comics.

I don't run into Arnold as much as I used to. I have chosen to slow my business affairs down and focus more on my revitalized "carpe diem" philosophy of life. Arnold hasn't slowed down a bit; in fact he's expanding his operation. This is understandable since he has three sons who will take over after him.

I arrived a little late, and I could see he was happy to see me, as I was him.

Arnold's wife of 42 years, Elyse, came over and gave me a big hug, then gave me the dickens about being such a stranger. I told her I would try and mend my ways.

Arnold, the boys, and I talked late into the night. The boys are just like their old man, blunt and to the point.

Institutions of higher education today teach young minds at such a high level of expertise that our well-educated young, who will determine and define the world, have grown up numb. I am not schooled about schools, yet I detect that the flow of purged mush and madness of asylums have poured into the bellies of the universities.

I recently found my answer concerning my convictions on this matter in the form of a book that should be canonized; *Illiberal Education*, by the Brahmin Dineesh D'Souza.

The world today is viewed by American youth in extremes: extreme expertise and extreme illusion. It's a delight to be around Arnold's boys, who missed out being indoctrinated in this manner.

I often see ranchers' sons behaving like diplomats, and it turns my stomach.

At breakfast, the boys talked about the Gulf war. Bush did well but didn't finish. The discovery of the extensive Iraqi nuclear weapons program looks to be a reprieve for the world, if only a temporary one.

Far too many souls for sale.

China leads Iran in the real dance as Pakistan smiles:

Muslims around the world await.

Nations are beginning to prepare for lives underground.

The economy is slipping deeper and deeper into a depression.

The difficult times can be a spiritual rejuvenation for many. There is no greater joy than looking into someone's eyes who is at home, but who has long been away.

Getting to bed late this evening. As I sleep I smell the lilacs and the lotus. I'm immersed in pure love, dancing a fast movement without body, but yet feeling the warm winds, and seeing the blue one above. I am India after the Aryans.

As I wake this morning, I cannot help but feel the pain of transcendence. I am certain that all through my day I will smell the lilac and lotus. Am I living in the midst of east Tennessee, or am I in the pink forest of the Punjab?

I'm taking Shorty for a ride into the hills this afternoon. It's cold today and overcast. The way I feel right now is worth the strife of 1000 lifetimes. I'd swear there are times I can see Ole Johnny Reb up here. I just hope I don't run into the 1st Illinois. I rode past an old still that was still smoking. Habits change slowly in these hills.

My ulcer has been acting up. Today I feel like I'm being eaten alive from the inside. Tonight's dinner will surely feed my sinister ulcer for weeks. I'm going to cook sausage and duck gumbo.

There's a used bookstore not too far from Vandy where I go to buy books when I'm in Nashville. I got this recipe from a cajun cookbook I bought there a while back.

I can feel the rumblings of a great battle waiting to be waged. All the soldiers who defend my food storage compartment have thrown their arms down and are now in full retreat. The hoards of sausage, duck, okra, and jalapeño have overrun my stomach. If there is a late night attack on my intestines, as I foresee, it could be a sleepless night. I was glad I put a skylight in my bathroom a few years ago. It is the place where comfort greets cosmos.

I read the book *Goldwater* this week.

"Extremism in the defense of liberty is no vice!"

Goldwater's words at the Republican National Convention in 1964 have been replaced by the Democratic slogan of our time, "Peace before Principle."

Chamberlainites in England in the 1930's, liberal Democrats in the United States in the 1970's and 1980's.

Ilysa called while I was away. She wants me to take her to the symphony in Nashville next week. She told me the *Russian Sailor's Dance* was on the program. She always knows how to cut right through me and get a yes. I'm glad the rest of humanity doesn't know me like she does.

The Russian composers are powerful and deep like their suffering.

Until very recently the Russians to my knowledge have never tasted freedom, and their music is an outcry. Even in the most oppressive of circumstances, creativity will ooze through, find its medium, have its orgasm and bring forth life.

I should sleep well tonight, since I didn't sleep last night. Oatmeal for dinner tonight and warm milk with a splash of Pepto for good measure.

God's knowledge of men is acquired through the knowledge of the night. When man is awake, God is asleep. But when man is asleep, God is listening.

I dreamt that colored threads ran from my mind up into the sky.

Confirmed with Ilysa for Saturday a week.

Created six new steers this morning. Castration goes against everything I feel inside. I've done it for years, but have never come to terms with it.

Creation appears to be in many pieces awaiting completion into the perfect idea. Einstein said, "I want to know God's thoughts." Einstein was of God's thoughts as is the drunkard and the stillborn.

I feel content late at night — it's the superficial feeling that I'm not being seen. Yet it's in the darkness that, underneath, I feel like I'm being penetrated, and skinned alive by the room of mirrors inside me. In this frame of thought, I passed into sleep.

I watched tall Dinka tribesmen pouring into the Sudan all broken from travel, starvation, and death. They came upon a group of nuns flying kites. The pious nuns took one look at the Dinka tribesmen and became enthused.

The nuns one by one took a Dinka tribesman and began to fly them as kites. To the nuns, the Dinka bodies were better than kites in negotiating the heavy winds. It was hard for me to understand this because I was kite string of one of the nuns, and thought the Dinka attached to me was heavy as lead. The winds picked up violently, like a ferocious bite. I became wrapped around an enormous church steeple that was unsteady and beginning to crack. I looked down below the clouds and saw the many bases of the steeple on earth coming under siege. The Dinka tribesman had become pinned around the steeple and was now face to face with the nun flying him who had been swept upwards. I held the two together until the steeple cracked. The nun fell to earth and died a violent death. The Dinka tribesman had held on to me and lowered himself down without incident.

Ilysa and the symphony are on my mind this morning. The wonderful thing about gazing into the future is that when it finally arrives, it's refreshingly different than what I had imagined it would be.

Insignificant revelations often make me feel like I am being tickled by God.

To look at those who spend their lives in laughter at nothingness seduces many minds to believe that reality is chaotic. Let the fools laugh and the unsure ponder, for they both add to the order of reality.

The verdict is always in the direction of principle.

Men can assimilate with themselves or others only

through the manifestation of principle.

The ascension by and between men in their adherence to principle is morality. Morals are but a theatrical mathematics where men have, more often than not, gotten lost in the theatrics, at the expense of the mathematics.

The idea of cultural assimilation has more often than not asked one to take refuge in another. A form of theatrics.

> *Moses pleaded: "Joseph's remains are taken*
> *into the land and I am not to enter?"*
> *And God replied: "Joseph asserted that he was*
> *a Hebrew." [Gen 39:14, 40:15] "Whereas you*
> *kept silent, when referred to as an Egyptian."*
> *[Ex. 2:19]*

Levi Deut R. 2.8.

It's been a good day, because my work has been efficient.

I pressed my shirt for the symphony. I put on way too much starch. My creases are sharp enough to cut bread, and hard enough to hit a Nolan Ryan fastball. Oh, well.

Except for the game with Alabama, Tennessee had a wonderful season. College football is a game that would have made the Spartans proud. Stormin' Norman even compared the Gulf War to a football play: an end-run. To me it looked more like a "red dog" with its ears pinned back. The Americans were the Miami Hurricanes and the Iraqis were Bob's Beauty College; we just let Bob get away.

It's a cold night here on my porch, as I sit here alone in my swing. I feel free because my porch is not a gulag or any other chamber of horrors. How can one not feel infinity when looking out into the stars, and not be grateful to the Creator of that infinity. My body withers around my soul that feels equal kinship with both infinitude and my sore aging shoulder, as I rock upon this rusted swing.

4:45 a.m. arrives quickly. I am nose-to-nose with Dali. I get up and we greet each other respectfully. My Saturdays are as long as the rest of the days of the week, although I usually occupy my time in frivolity.

My date with Ilysa is at 7:00 p.m., and I feel like a fidgety teenager.

Ilysa is a Jewess from Bavaria who was the only one in her immediate family to survive the war. History has disrupted her internal bearings and left her like a duck on a dry lake, neither swimming nor flying high. To me, Ilysa is royalty.

Ilysa looked stunning and the Russian marches and sonatas made this Saturday evening almost romantic for me. This age is not a delicate age. Tonight's music felt peacefully anachronistic.

I took the back roads home from Nashville. As I have gotten older, there are fewer and fewer farms.

I got home about 1:30 a.m. I sat on the porch until about 3:00 a.m., listening to the silence.

I dreamt that I was driving a truck through a desert in mountain country. I looked very tan. The road looked familiar, and even the odd gear ratio on the truck looked familiar.

It's snowing this morning.

After I finish my coffee, I'm going to go over to the Robson hospital and visit the kids in the cancer ward.

I don't know what first moved me to come out here, but I've been coming about twice a month for 2 years. My visits are always fun and tragic. A kid I was fond of died during the week, Bobby Jay McAllen, age 8.

He was an orphan.

He knew his fate.

His parents didn't want him but the earth did.

The doctors and nurses knew he was a kid with a special insight. He had a quiet resolve in him that permitted him to laugh mockingly at the nurses from time to time. Once I witnessed this. How strange it was, when Bobby smiled back at me. I felt as though I was the child and he the adult. I'll miss him.

I walked through the AIDS corridor today. In all my life I had never seen grown men suffer so. I don't understand why these loaded guns are not quarantined. If they do not walk away now, many will fall away tomorrow. I am convinced that this plague, that has yet to fully strike, is a punishment from heaven.

Moral relativism is a front that has become a license to stand against the Law.

Behavior immune to morals begets the death sentence by the absence of immunity as executioner.

The United States is an AIDS patient.

The Blacks believe themselves to be of the first and of the last. Perhaps. Perhaps not. I cannot see humanity in Africa soon, or thriving Africans elsewhere, because this plague will garner the Africans no quarter.

June left me a message today; she wants to have lunch this week. Between Ilysa and June, I'm mothered to death, but I wouldn't have it any other way.

This morning I feel empty space moving in conjunction with the rotation of planets in my mind. It gazed out at my imagination, its creation, and wondered.

I dropped off 1/2 cord of wood at Jr. Wilcox's this morning. I traded him the wood for preserves and pecans. Jr. is my bartering partner. Last month I traded him a TV for a freezer full of venison.

When the economy collapses in this country, those who are left in the country will do business by bartering.

The people of these hills won't feel the economic collapse near as much as those in the cities who rely on paper money and credit cards.

The bartering between us over the years has brought me some of my fondest memories. I don't remember one time that my company with Jr. was ever void of lunacy. I have seen everything in Jr.'s yard from pink minks to

Sherman tanks, not only on the same day, but in the same damn transaction. Whenever we speak I am the recipient of current adventures that would make any Hollywood comedy appear as chicanery.

This afternoon there's a ceremony for some young men getting into the lodge.

The lodge is a cheerful place of moral men. I'm overcome with a feeling of calm, when I enter the lodge. This is one of the few places that I have ever been where a group of men are content as they are and who they are. My brethren here are not on the road to becoming something; they have all arrived long ago.

It is this quality in the simple man that is so resented by the men of the liberal establishment, because they know they will never attain it in themselves. This is so because the process of attaining it requires capacities for introspection, confrontation, shame, and most of all, an acquired faith through action. The modern American liberal flutters hopelessly in the make-believe world of externality.

He lacks a discipline for the sound principles of prevention. He is too smug even to be inspired.

The liberal of this day and age in the United States is a confused, entangled spirit who views evil men merely as misguided children. He holds this view because he is afraid of the misgivings in his own nature. He is terrified of punishment because it resonates with those weaknesses in his own nature that haunt him in his days and in his nights. The greatest fear of the modern American liberal would be to expose his faithless character. His so-called "love-for-mankind" theme is in reality a desperate over-compensation conceived in fear. The truth behind this theme of the modern American liberal is a desperate yearning to be loved himself, as he exists in his own terrified state. Basically, what he is saying is, "Through putting up with me, please try to love me, even though I am trying to destroy and dismantle the noble things in your world."

In the myth of Robin Hood, Robin the Saxon stole from John the Norman, not for the poor but to ransom King Richard the Lion-Hearted, his political ally.

I enjoyed today very much. It was good to see the boys in the lodge. My feelings of sentimentality were short lived because I began to think about the economy.

Today, the United States is in a depression that hasn't fallen off the cliff yet.

We have shipped our jobs elsewhere and been dumped on by others through unfair trade policies. Our products are shoddy, the military industrial complex is a monster for corruption, the government has become one large social and regulatory agency, the legal establishment is stealing all it can get its hands on, our cities are fading into anarchy, money has become a commodity thus making the nation a nation of money changers, our politicians are self-serving orators whose only focus is victory in their next election, and we're headed for a race war.

Will Durant wrote,

A nation is born Stoic, and dies Epicurean.[15]

Alexandr I. Solzhenitsyn, *The Gulag Archipelago:*

*Even the chief of some provincial NKVD admin-
istration, if some sort of mess developed, could
show Stalin his hands were clean . . . he had
issued no direct instructions to use torture! But
at the same time, he had insured that torture
would be used!*[16]

Colonel John S. Mosby in *Partisan Life* said it best
when he said,

*For they are held together by the cohesive power
of public plunder.*[17]

The American conservative performs misdeeds with
more confidence than does the American liberal. The
wrongdoings of the Conservative tend to be through
more established channels, where he can hide behind
histories.

The conservative/liberal debate is often a deflective. Its
continual theatrics holds the attention of the many who,
were it not for this charade, would be following more
closely the exchange of monies flowing in and out of the
right and left hands.

There is no trust.

With seven years of famine ahead, those of the left and of the right do not atone, but continue to gawk.

They believe that plugging in this measure or that will subdue decades of aspiritual policy.

It is the little things by the many and the big things by the few that have set in motion a pattern for the fall of this nation.

Virtue underlies everything.

To focus directly on economics is to worship a false god.

Today's government doesn't seem to understand that you can't spend yourself into prosperity.

Every item the U.S. government overpays for, be it ten cents on a hammer or the overpaid salary of a bureaucrat, infringes upon the freedom of the citizenry.

Governments never seem to understand that more can be accomplished by freedom than by control.

The absence of freedom breeds in the citizenry an aversion to risk that leaves great spirits unfulfilled.

As a result, we are left with lesser prophets and devils instead of greater prophets and kings.

It is difficult to petition for freedom when so many are already so oppressed by freedom.

Government should provide for self defense and adjudicate disputes between its members, leaving all else to the interplay of the citizenry. A Christian man I know recently said to me the following:

_It says in the Christian Testament, 'What you do
unto the least of these, you do unto me.' FDR gave
this statement his own interpretation when he
said, 'A chicken in every pot.' These two state-
ments have come to say the same thing as a referendum upon public policy in America that says, 'If
you have something and somebody else doesn't
have it, then give it to them!' FDR supplemented
the family unit with the government. Since the
government is dysfunctional, therefore we are the
children of a dysfunctional family._

To force men to give is to rob them of their volition to
give, and it embitters them.

To force men to give beyond their means, as is the case
in America today through excessive taxes, is tyrannical.

Why there was never an amendment to the Constitution that called for a balanced budget, I'll never know.

Today it's too late because the patient is already
terminally ill and would die on the table.

I helped Earl Bussey frame up a barn this morning.
Framing in the winter goes much slower than in the
summer. As I think about the work I've done in my life,
I feel blessed that my working arrangements allowed me
personal freedom and independence.

By the end of the day, Earl's barn looked like a big
dinosaur skeleton. It was a sight to see the light of a cold
dusk shooting through it. The broken light sprayed the

back of an adjacent hillside bringing to life an assortment of random branches and flowers.

Seeing the flowers reminded me that I'm having lunch with June tomorrow.

We always go to Ma Fignons. Ma runs an old boarding house where she serves lunch during the week. I never knew either of my grandmothers, but if I had, I'm sure a lot of Ma would be recognizable in them both.

Ma and June have been close for a very long time. Ma and Emmy, June's mother, were also very close, and when Emmy died, Ma, June's godmother, stepped in to raise her.

Ma is a strong, intelligent, and opinionated woman and a pure intuitionist. Her honesty is always rough and ready.

Ma, June and I were in a heated debate one evening, about what I don't remember. Anyway, Ma hit her boiling point and said, "Karl, you're a cantankerous stiff-necked Jew!" I responded to Ma by relating to her a quip that I had heard by chance earlier in the day. God's greatest achievement on the earth was France, then God thought a second . . . "maybe I'd better trash France up a bit so the other nations don't get jealous . . ." so God created Frenchmen.

(Ma was in her late 70's at the time.) She walked across the porch, jumped in my lap, and kissed me on the lips, dentures and all. There were about 12 people on the porch that night, and not one of them lent a hand to get

Ma out of my lap or off my face. When I finally did get her off, she pulled out her dentures, then looked me dead in the eye and said, "Karl, your restlessness is because you are a Jew, and it costs you any chance of love."

I felt a venom running through me that began to overcome my nervous system. I couldn't look at anyone, especially June. I got up and walked home alone.

Walking home, I avoided self-pity and thought about her cutting words. Whether love has escaped me in this life or I have escaped it, it is hard to judge. I didn't marry June because she could not seduce away my heart from my God. Her god is not my God. I chose heaven over love.

Today, Ma is in her 90's. She has lost most of her fiery wit, partly because of old age, and partly because of wisdom. She lights up when June and I show up for lunch. She always takes us both by the hand and walks us into the sun parlor where we chat.

From time to time, she forgets where she is and begins speaking in French. Last week she lapsed into her mother tongue, and began to weep. I had never seen her weep before. I wrote down what she kept saying between her tears:

Mais, le chemin du droit est, comme la lumére de l'aube, qui brille toujours plus pendant la parfalte journeé. Le chemin des mauvais est comme le ténebre ils ne savent pas contre quoi il vont cogner.

Words with a meaning so far away.

I wanted to ask her about these words, but deep down I felt it would be an intrusion.

I met June at Ma's at noon. I smelled like hay, but looked relatively nice considering the work I had done since 5:00 a.m. June was wearing a tweed jacket and grey skirt that made her look like the Queen of Scots. Ma as always took us into the sun parlor after lunch. She swallowed a glass of cognac and seemed to thoroughly enjoy it.

Ma is a woman of rare glimpses. From the recesses of her ancient mind she speaks out without any apparent reason, intent, or direction, yet she transmits from holiness to holiness.

Today she said, "The ones who haven't been broken do much of the breaking, and those who have been or are broken and know, do the quiet rebuilding."

The true man or woman of heart is more often than not awkward of speech and a clumsy outcast when compared with the slicker men of words.

Isserlein Pesakim 1519

Many are ordained but few know.[18]

Moses could barely speak a lick, but he could kill an Egyptian with his hands and build cities.

June and I saw Ma tiring so we called it a day. I kissed them both goodbye, then left.

Driving home I realized like never before how strong my kinship with Ma really is. She sees.

By the grace of her quiet does she write the molds for the seals of the mystical legalities.

She smiles with the soft confidence of one who only could have been gathered in by the angels of resolve.

I got home, took a hot shower, sat down in my chair and looked down at Dali. He looked up at me, and I knew that inside he was smiling like a clown. He began to lick my leg as if it were a bowl of red-eye gravy. I got up and filled his bowl with some beef stew that I made the day before. Dali ate with the quiet and grace of a bulldozer moving concrete, so I went in my bedroom and flipped on the news.

There is a death threat on the Islamic writer Salaman Rushdie.

Overcoming insecurity and monopolization in thought where all thought is considered personal and threatening, not independent and differentiated, will be mankind's greatest cognitive task in the next century.

What is evil and what is good?

What is sacred and what is not sacred? All lay together in living tombs of dead youth.

I just watched myself drown in my dream. It has taken me many years of concentration to watch a death in my dreams. It is only a temporal death of individual form; an unveiling.

Interesting conversation at Barkey's this morning. A couple of Europeans who are traveling across America joined our breakfast group. One was a Finn, and the other a Swede. We talked politics with them for a bit.

I told them that in spite of its past greatness, the United States is in the process of breaking apart.

An institutional Constitution, no matter how noble, cannot be maintained by those with no perspective for the noble and honorable life, that should rest within themselves first as individual constitutions.

When men defecate on paper, call it art, demand that I pay for it with my taxes, and are getting away with it, I am left with little hope for this future land of the native.

When art is not a communal blessing, it is an individual curse.

The two Europeans watched TV in perplexity a few minutes, as Uncle "Teeny" laughed at their perplexity. Uncle "Teeny" pointed at the TV, and said, "They create for their own image."

"They purport to deflect."

"They are all so damned empty inside."

Freedom is not always its own antiseptic.

There are many in the land who yearn to clean and to reclaim.

I came in the house this afternoon and the phone was ringing. It was June. She was crying. She said Ma had died about an hour ago, and that the funeral was tomorrow.

Death is always a shock. I'm now left with a vacuum in my life. Where there was once a magical forest where I used to play, there are now only memories. Replacing philosophy for passion in moments of duress makes my body both the battlefield and the casualty as I make the transition from shock to reflection.

As I lay down to sleep, in my heart of hearts I was weeping for Ma. However, the philosophy in my mind prevented any tears from reaching my eyes.

Ma appeared before me briefly and she was wearing a coat of many colors. This was all I needed to see to know that she was all right.

Ma's funeral would be at St. Mary's, the only Catholic church in Robson.

I don't know if Ma would have approved of this or not.

Ma spoke to me concerning her death only once. She said, "I have grown weary from being a witness in a world where many refuse to testify."

Coming into St. Mary's the young priest, whom I had never seen before, called me aside and asked me to be a pallbearer. It seems Ma had made a few confessions in her last hours.

I asked the priest if Ma had come back to her faith, and he said that she had not.

From dust to dust.

I want to get drunk tonight. I drank some ulcer medicine to coat my stomach, then followed with half a bottle of Chivas.

The room is spinning and God has turned his back on me in disgust. Even Dali has left me. When a man even for a moment leaves himself, as now, the world becomes blind to who he is. Pre-meditated escape into blind

drunkenness is neither virtuous nor moral but necessary for the one who is down but whose eyes are open.

I awoke disoriented but refreshed. No breakfast this
morning, although I have a terrible craving for grits, as
they always seem to soothe my stomach after a night of
drink.

Loading hay bales and hung-over this morning is a
physical confession.

This morning's self-initiated physical confession was
not a diatribe.

A Catholicism that continues to render the confession
as a method to absolve responsibility illegitimatizes
itself.

The Catholic Church's use of confession is a means and
method of control. It's a way to keep the people, unthink-
ing, irresponsible and dependent. Individual shame
relinquished into the corporate is profanity. Moments of
shame are sacred in the same way that dung is the source
of growth.

Catholicism with great zest and candles instructs its
true believers that rewards are found in the next life.

Catholicism fails to see the spirit of the earth as an
epoch of God's lair.

Much work to be done this afternoon. Repairing the
fence on my western slope should take most of it. I've
never cared for barbed-wire. I remember seeing a North
Korean who was so entangled in it that he bled to death.
Running barbed-wire is like trying to break a mule, you

just work with it and hope for the best.

I think what Ma will miss most from life is laughter. What quality in the rapturous perfection of heaven could possibly replace side-splitting laughter? Heaven is probably so holy and balanced that exaggerations cannot penetrate, so they just fall hopelessly to earth, where we look upon them and think that they are real.

5:00 a.m. I am consumed in sweat. I have been turning over and over in my bed since midnight or even earlier. There is misery in the space between the two worlds of wake and sleep. It is a finite space of distractions that are forever masking each other, only to be born anew, and nothing with a conscience can deny itself an encounter with a newborn.

It's 35 degrees and raining this morning. I walk outside naked, and stand in the rain for a minute or two. I'm awake now. What an invigorating response to a night that had me battling for sleep, a battle in which I was soundly defeated. My shower this morning is a pretentious gesture.

I couldn't sleep last night because I was thinking about the point of coherence that links the physical and spiritual worlds into one. One night while I was dreaming, the answer came to me from a source outside of myself. The answer was posed mathematically, composed of numbers representing spirit and formulas representing matter. I saw the equations moving in and out of each other and it was correct in every movement.

Breakfast conversation this morning was about cattle prices. I was pretty silent this morning. I was content to just drink my coffee and listen. Avery Bishop asked me if we could pick up his feed at noon instead of this morning, since he had to go to Nashville and pick up his Florida lottery tickets. I said fine, but I want 10% of the winnings. He said 5%, and I said 9%; he said 7% and I said OK. Avery never got past the eighth grade, but I bet he could out hustle any Arab market trader or riverboat gambler. He's worth about 12 million, and worked for every dollar.

Avery is an unusually generous man. In 1960, when the first Robson hospital was being built, the city was having trouble raising capital. An anonymous check for a million dollars found its way into the city treasurer's office, and the hospital was completed and staffed ahead of schedule. Many believe that it was Avery who gave the money, but he's always denied it. A month after the hospital opened, Avery had a heart attack. Had the medics tried to drive him to Nashville, I'm told he would have died. In Avery's case the correlation between charity and providence was profound. Avery has yet to receive a hospital bill from Robson General in over 30 years.

My afternoon with Avery was pleasant. His hopes for winning the lottery are childlike in their innocence and wonderment. His feelings rubbed off on me this afternoon and now at dusk I feel lofty in thought and giddy in temperament.

My television is on the blink and I couldn't be happier. I like the silence.

Eternity, from all I can deduce, will be silent, and the silence will make it blissful.

I am unsure if there is transformation and change in eternity.

Arthur Schopenhauer hypothesized that death retrieves one to the place that one was before birth.

As I slept, I began to weep. When I was a small child, my parents had blessed me with a younger brother who died at age two in an auto accident. I saw him bleed to death. My parents never overcame this. I loved young Max, and I have often wondered about him, who he would have been, what he would have looked like, what he might have thought.

Looking upward at the moon and at the dawn, I remember a strange but wonderfully imaginative article I read a few years ago in a physics journal. It stated that if time travel were possible, it would work in the following way: One would have to exit or step out of the universe, only to re-enter at another point. What would it be that could divide one universe from another? I have often in my life applied this question as an analogy between men, as I think of my brother who was not to be.

Breakfast this morning was pretty ordinary until Betty Anne Downes walked through the door. Betty Anne was my first. I got up and walked over to her table and said hello. We talked a few minutes and laughed a bit. I said you know that you were my first, and she said you were my first "Karl." She lives in Louisville but was home for a few days to visit her mother. She was leaving to catch a plane right after breakfast. Before we parted she said, "Karl, I always knew you would remain here because you've always acted as though Robson was your stepchild that needed care and guidance." I didn't know quite what she meant by that.

Reggie called today and wished me a happy birthday. He said his wife Emily had baked me a birthday cake, and that I should hurry over. Standing with Reggie and his family in the front yard, we ate cake and watched the most horrific lightning storm that I have ever seen.

June called tonight and said to meet her at Ma's tomorrow evening at 6:30 p.m.

Tomorrow I'll take Dali to stud Priscilla in Blackstone. If he only knew the glories that awaited him.

Hear, O Israel, the Lord our God,
the Lord is One.

My mother would say these words to me at my bedside before I went to sleep. She told me never to forget them. My relationship with the Jewish God for all of my years has been turbulent but unscathed in its commitment. Yet, I am perplexed that I have such an exceedingly difficult time getting on with my co-religionists.

I continue to learn much from the prophets of the Hebrew Bible, Spinoza, and ben Maimon, yet I rarely if ever read modern Jewish writers. Far too many of them wander about aimlessly in the shadows of the enormous spiritual failures of the Diaspora; and with failed tools, no less.

Oh, Lord, I see thee in the canvas of the sky, I hear thee in the music of my dreams, I feel thee when the leaf falleth unto my skin in the dead of winter when there are no leaves.

A prayer from a spiritual pragmatist like myself should please God, since he too knows how to work well with his hands.

Rudman of Gramm-Rudman is walking away in disgust. These two represent the very best that we have now.

Many in the land have come to think about and smile upon Ross Perot, because he could be the reprieve. There will be no reprieve.

In the recent election in Israel (June 1992), the fearful Jews elected their new Chamberlain (Rabin) against their Churchill (Shamir).

How people love to live in lies.

The opinions of the press and public were in no way founded upon reality; but the adverse tide was strong.

In this dark time the basest sentiments received acceptance or passed unchallenged by the responsible leaders of the political parties"[19]

Winston Spencer Churchill
The Gathering Storm

If Alexis de Tocqueville crossed this land today and wrote of it, his words would be a eulogy.

All the innocence has been drained away, as the worms feast.

The sound of my mother's voice often calls out to me, as I lay down to sleep. Even in my 60th year, I am still my mother's child. Six months ago I bought two wooden statues of what looked to be an old East European peasant couple. A month after I purchased them, I was rummaging through my mother's trunk and found hidden under some old letters, this same old couple in wood.

When I was a child, my mother would read me poetry as I would imagine living in the softness of Renoir's paintings. When I see his paintings now, I am overcome with a feeling to cloak myself in a purple velvet cape and swim through the clouds until I reach France of a century ago where the emancipations of simplicity were at their height, and where the Epicureans perfected the subtleties of their craft.

I awoke peacefully this morning; I worked, had breakfast, then loaded Dali into my truck. I feel anxious for him, almost like a father feels for his son who will experience love for the first time. The entire trip, I couldn't keep my eyes off Dali. He looks into space like he created it, in contrast with people who look into space so often with such pronounced fear and anxiety.

The South African Whites chose to bring the Blacks into their government by referendum. In doing so, the Whites have taken on an ocean of humanity completely at odds with their passions for order. The White South Africans have opted for a slow death.

The many different nations are scrambling to return to their beginnings. Before there will be togetherness, there will be separateness.

We pulled up to Ione Profits' house. Ione owns Priscilla. Ione is a very nice and polite woman, a true daughter of the Confederacy. She said to leave Dali for a few days until the consummation of the marriage is physically and spiritually completed. I looked at Ione and told her that I now thought she was one of my in-laws. She laughed and said she felt the same way. I told her to take good care of my son, and daughter-in-law, and that I'd be back in a few days.

The tobacco shop where I buy tobacco replaced its dirty magazine section with flowers. This left me feeling hopeful.

I walked into Ma's for the first time since her death. June handed me a letter dated August 2nd 1943. She pointed to the bottom of the page where it said,

*Mais, le chemin du droit est, comme la lumére
de l'aube, qui brille toujours plus pendant la
parfalte journeé. Le chemin des mauvais est
comme le ténebre ils ne savent pas contre quoi il
vont cogner.*

I remembered these words from Ma's alzheimer's
poetry reading in her parlour shortly before her death.
The letter was in French, but June had it translated.

*But the path of the righteous is as the light of
dawn that shineth more and more unto the
perfect day. The way of the wicked is as darkness; they know not at what they stumble.*

The Hebrew Bible

The letter was from a desperate priest in Prague telling
Ma that her younger sister, a nun under his service had
been executed.

So much of life is hidden.

I drove home from Ma's thinking about King Saul.

He fell from grace because he hearkened to the cries of
a frightened people. Moses acted the same way when he
struck the rock for water.

This century has produced men of unbreakable will
whose ideals, no matter what the cost in human life,
always took precedence. The quality so yearned for by a
hopeful and jealous God has been most pronounced in

this century by the destroyers.

The openness of the sky tonight extends over the earth like a drape that ties far below the bottom of the earth in a hangman's noose waiting to be used.

As I slept, I entered a world of fallen soldiers. I spoke with Spartans, Persians, Mesopotamians, Germans, and Americans. All were faceless, but their uniforms were all well kept.

When I awoke the next morning, I walked over to my closet and looked at my Marine Corps dress greens, from Korea; the creases are still sharp.

The Charlie Daniels' Band was playing on the jukebox this morning. Charlie Daniels was singing a song that was a tribute to Americans. He sang, "You just lay your hands on a Pittsburg Steeler fan." Well, I've been a Steeler fan all of my life, and when I heard those words, I could just see the Immaculate Reception all over again.

(The very near future)

*Part II
Israel*

The world economy is in a depression rampant with famine.

The famines of Africa have caught the rest.

There is no quiet dying by the new starving, but madness, vengance, and war.

They have not known of minds, spirits, or winds, but only of accumulation.

Breaking and breaking apart reign as death pangs and as birth pangs.

The crumbling of the body (the nation state) begins in the mind.

There were many that didn't trust the rest.

In not trusting the rest, they found that they couldn't trust themselves.

In feeling their feelings, I felt they thought of the many

who were not like themselves as vile. They thought that the vile ones were too stupid to understand the higher truths, while they lied about the lower truths. They gathered in gold and power at the expense of those they thought were vile.

The American Blacks have opened the prisons in the land and freed their bretheren, indifferent towards their guilt and because there is no more food.

Europe is battling to expel all third-world peoples from its continent.

Europe is Germany.

The dispersion from Babel intensifies homeward, through its second self, as China thinks.

The collapse of the U.S. economy was precipitated in large part by the collapse of the Savings and Loans and the banking system. The old men that ran these institutions operated by the ole saying, "It's somebody else's money." They squandered the savings of the nation that it took years to amass.

Nations crumble when the people do not believe in anything.

Justice in the United States in the end came to mean "just us."

This once greatest of all nations, with a Constitution that could have only been brought forth by the will of heaven, is no more.

The United States was an experiment by heaven that sought to transform the ways of men, by providing them with a home governed under principle.

It was the ultimate house of worship.

It was the temple of the West that fell. Now the land is without Constitution and without name. The United States were more truly the states of being united.

The framers of the union were of the best and brightest that heaven had ever produced.

Prophets.

Humanity has become an afflicted Job but without soul, lying far from the understanding.

Billy Williams knocked on my door this evening. I haven't seen my peer preacher in many years. He said to me, "Karl, it's time for you to go." I knew where his thoughts were. Jews from all over the globe were returning to Israel. It is the return as predicted in the book of Isaiah:

> For though thy people, O Israel, be as the sand of the sea, only a remnant of them shall return; and it shall come to pass in that day, that the Lord will set His hand again the second time to recover the remnant of His people, and He will set up an ensign for the nations, and will assemble the dispersed of Israel, and gather together the scattered of Judah from the four corners of the earth.

American farmers, fishermen, and entrepreneurs are no longer free.

The independent businessman, has been overrun, along with his independence.

Let the dreamers dream about a world without walls, but as a Jew who can't find a market for either his crop or his cattle in a starving world, I realize that I too must go with the rest.

All over the globe former Americans will take the lessons of America unto their new lands to clean, to order and to make right.

I've found the news of the return to be pretty accurate in *The Economist*. Three million Jews have immigrated to Israel from all over the globe in the last year and half, and can be found living in massive tent cities spread out all over the country. I find the whole event extraordinary.

In the past, the Israelis would only accept Jews from somewhere else if they consented to work for free and live like socialists. Maggie Thatcher said the British are too proud a race to be socialists. Israel's socialism has until now kept the Western Jews in the West.

The Western Jews paid while the Israelis fought. Soon both will pay and both will fight.

I dread this move as much as anything I've ever had to do in my whole life. I'm going into the womb of a people I admire but don't understand, and in the most adverse of circumstances.

The United States has come to an end, but its Constitution will live with humanity forever.

All I have left is a suitcase and a plane ticket.

Ilysa is in Jerusalem with her cousin, and Dali died last year. I'm glad I didn't take one of his pups, because if I had, I might not go now. June will take me to the airport in the morning.

The drive with June to Nashville was solemn. We knew that we'd never see each other again.

In leaving the United States I look over my shoulder for one last glimpse at the White man of America.

His race and his Christianity are doomed.

Conditions even in rural America are unbearable as anarchy rages.

Mountain towns and unseen crevices have magnetized the White into anxious enclaves.

The darker ones do not chase, but shall catch the Whites.

Final solutions are for nature to decide.

I kissed June good-bye, and told her how very much I loved her, and we parted.

From this day forward, I decided I wouldn't shave.

I could feel my life-long manicured Southern instincts being replaced at least in physical form by the need to ascend into the role of a Semitic mystic, a transformation of being not unlike that of Gandhi or Aurobindo.

Like John Barth says, "It's only me in a sense."[20]

The Nashville airport was buzzing as the violent race wars in the country have made many in the populace look elsewhere for greener pastures.

I sat in the terminal next to a couple of men. One was

going to Dublin, and the other was going to Prague. They asked me where I was going, and I told them. The one going to Dublin said, "We're all going to homes we'd never been to." We wished each other well, then parted ways.

Kennedy airport was upon me. I collected my luggage and headed for the El Al terminal. My flight was scheduled for 1:55 p.m.

The terminal was a madhouse. I was approached continually for my ticket, but I didn't sell.

I was told time and again by strangers in the terminal how very lucky I was to have a ticket. I didn't feel very lucky.

In the terminal I ran into a Jew, who was a Southern planter. He was a wealthy aristocrat who wasn't squeamish about his traditions and biases. In speaking with him, I was gratified to finally meet a Jew who refused to give in and call a duck a donkey or a duck an eagle when in fact a duck is a duck and an eagle is an eagle, and a donkey is most certainly still a donkey.

I finally boarded at about 7:10 p.m.; it has been a long and unsettling day.

I was fortunate to get an aisle seat in the back, where I wouldn't feel like a sardine.

I sat next to a couple of teenagers and their father. They looked to be Israeli and were. I talked with the kids a few minutes. I didn't communicate well with them. Their thoughts were not grounded in anything I felt to be important.

I had felt that the socialist system in Israel would be transformed to a capitalist one not by American Jews, but more so by the Israelis who had left Israel for the West and were now forced to return. After speaking with these kids and their father, I'm not so sure.

I napped for a couple of hours and was awakened by a stewardess who was serving dinner.

Dali's death was at the right time and in the right manner, but I longed to see his big brown eyes looking up at my dinner.

The exodus in the 1930's was being relived here in the 1990's.

The diaspora for the Jews is over.

The true believers around me that are now lost in their singing will awaken abruptly when they hit the tent cities in the desert and are stifled and blocked by the Israeli bureaucracy when they are told there's no toilet paper.

The Jew need not fool himself with respect to the diaspora. It was a punishment, and a damned harsh one, brought down because the Jew didn't know how to behave in his own land.

Other peoples who misbehave often become extinct. The return of the Jews, as well as the return of others, is a metahistorical act of removing blindfolds.

People began to move about the plane, as I just watched. There was a traffic jam between my aisle and an adjacent aisle. A woman was trying to get her daughter from her husband so she could get her to the bathroom. They were having difficulty, so I lifted the little girl on my shoulders, and with my 250 pounds cleared the way so the little girl could appease mother nature. The mother was shocked and delighted; I was just happy to keep the floor under my feet dry.

I sat back down in my seat and lifted up the bottom of my old work boot and saw between the cracks a small piece of a cow chip. I scraped it out, and rubbed it away between my thumb and little finger.

I slept until sunrise.

The sun pouring through my window woke me up. Today is one of the few days in my adult life that I didn't get up to go to work. The people around me began to sing again. I prefer the melody of a hammer driving nails.

I peered downwards and took a look at Ben Gurion Airport. It looked like Neyland Stadium on a Saturday afternoon right after a game, but the major difference is that the mass of people below me have no homes, and are not where they are by choice. I wondered where I'd fit in down there.

I went into an arrival area where I was interviewed, inspected, and given a physical—Ellis Island of another place and time.

I was given an identity badge and a bunk in the stadium. I would be here for two nights; then I would be transferred to the tent city in the desert.

The cattle car that I was on was packed with Jews from France. An Israeli came on the truck and said that the driver was sick, and could anyone here drive the truck? "All you have to do is to follow the truck in front of you." I said that I would drive. The truck had a strange gear ratio, that I had seen before, but for the moment, I couldn't remember where. The drive to the desert would be about one hundred miles. I feel like Ralph Kramden.

The drive made me feel like a modern day Bedouin. I would look back in my mirror from time to time and look at the Jews from France, all distraught. The Holocaust to them must be pure abstraction. I spoke to an Algerian Jew sitting next to me. I pointed to a camel on the road and asked him if it brought back memories of Algeria. He looked at the camel then looked at me and said, "It does."

Our Israeli guide or stewardess on the cattle car sitting behind me said, "It's a long drive to the Negev." I said, "Honey, I've been on bigger cattle ranches." She just smiled back at me in confusion. Her name is Hayalet, and she is a Yeminite about twenty. Her army uniform makes her look like a big Brownie.

I saw the tent city from the mountain road. It was itself at the foot of a mountain. I wonder what golden calves are being dreamt about down there? Looking at the Jews from the view, I think about Moses. Only Moses and Hitler could lead them.

I got my only suitcase and was shuffled into a make-shift army building where we were briefed.

The city was drastically short of everything, but the

Jews are a civilized people, so in spite of all the confusion and mayhem, I nevertheless felt this was a relatively safe place. I was shuffled off to the southern-most sector of the city, section H-40.

When I arrived, I was met by an army major who assigned me a bunk and issued me an I.D. card, food chits, toiletry chits, etc., etc.

I got to my bunk towards the rear and on the northern-most wall of the tent. I remembered that I had packed two fifths of sour mash in my suitcase. I broke the seal on one of the bottles and began to drink. I finished half the bottle and staggered out into the desert. I never realized how cold it gets in the desert at night. I understand but don't care for all the hullabaloo.

The Jew is escapist and discontented.

I can feel the enormous mystical power of heaven directing the events here.

Whiskey is a great way to meet people, but lousy for remembering them. I walked through the row of tents like a drunken rat through a maze. When I got back to my tent, all was dark and everyone was asleep, so I crawled into my rack and drifted into oblivion.

I dreamt that I saw the prophetess Deborah and she was screaming at me in desperation to come out, but I didn't. Like a drunken coward, I hid my face. She was surrounded by the corpses of dogs who were tortured by men, and who were being eaten by gentle dogs with excuses. Fearing for my life, I awoke. The subtlest subtleties crush the sleeping or momentarily complacent soul.

I awoke this morning at 5:00 a.m.; it is dark as pitch. Everyone in the tent was asleep. I could smell the mess tent and headed right towards it. I was greeted by a soldier at the entrance to the tent who wanted to see my meal chit. He told me to come back at 7:15 a.m.

On the way back, I saw a group of old men lecturing each other violently. I asked if they wouldn't mind me sitting and listening; after all, I didn't have any farm to run today. These men, as they explained to me, and as I deduced, were studying the Talmud. I listened for awhile.

The Law is simple, and simply written. All this excessive argument is a mockery.

What's good for the goose is good for the gander.

The state of Israel doesn't have the death penalty, yet the Holy Book states very simply that the death penalty should be enforced under certain conditions.

In light of Jewish history, I found this whole exercise of so-called "religious study" excessive and unsound. It's no accident that an entire generation of Talmudists was lost in WW II. They were purged because their faith was in nothing earned. They were without their own thoughts by their own minds with their own hands concerning their own lives.

Until holocaust and pogroms become hypothetical, I will continue to learn my religious lessons from the callouses on my hands.

An old blind man next to me who also just sat and listened asked me if I would walk him to his tent, and then he would make us some tea. I accepted. He moved silently and gracefully for a man without eyes. We drank our tea as the sun came up. He asked me to describe the sun rising and I did so. He smiled as I talked; then I fell silent, and we both just sat quietly.

I moved on to my tent, and the sun was now up. Close to a million people were beginning to move about. When I got back to my tent, the young children were up and running around. The ten men of my tent and I were to have a meeting at 9:00 a.m. All the men in my tent were American, and all between the ages of 28 and 40. I was the eldest.

I got to the chow hall at my allotted time. There were no eggs, bacon, potatoes, grits, or even coffee, just tomatoes and cucumbers.

The men in the tent wanted to get their families into more urban settings like Tel Aviv or Haifa. They felt uneasy in the wilderness. I didn't think that there was much of a difference. As a matter of fact, I even liked being away from civilization, or at least being on the verge of creating a new one.

I listened to the men go back and forth about their options as to where they would go, and what they would do. I told them that as long as they had food in their mouths and a tent over their heads for themselves and their families there was little reason to worry. Things could be a hell of a lot worse.

The wise man that lapses from time to time into fear shouldn't murmur as he awaits heaven's command.

As I look at the trauma that is afflicting these men, I think back to the book of Job.

Job was able to take from his overwhelming anxiety and fear the correct notion that perplexity is accepted as the most immediate and truest of realities.

I explained to them that settlements were going up as fast as possible, and that their turn would come to have a home again.

The Arabs and the Christians, along with their off-shoots, shall soon be expelled from Israel, along with their houses of worship that have served us only as an enemy.

The Druze may remain as honored guests as well as others like them that share the cost.

Israel's political system is a mosaic of ideologies all to the left and to the lesser left.

Europe has come together as a family to forge a defense against the darker ones and against the Oriental.

Europe mourns the loss of the United States to the darker ones while underneath it mourns for itself, knowing its fate will be the same.

Germany's awakening frightens Europe. Awakenings in Europe that frighten will pale in comparison with China's eventual awakening.

White slavery that has been so active in South America for so many years has now become prevalent on all continents.

Europe will attempt to sacrifice Israel into the belly of the third world by making an alliance with the East to save itself.

Europe will attempt to divide an unsure Israel by cornering her with talk of peace, thus dividing Israel into quarrelsome quarters.

Camp David was a Jewish Little Big Horn in diplomacy that the Europeans hope to use as a model for its future diplomatic relations with Israel.

The enemies of Israel know that the Jews are an insecure people wanting more than anything else to be accepted, and will pay any price for this acceptance, including their existence.

The Jews (the oldest race on the planet) run around the globe trying to court others' favor in order that others should recognize them. It's damned disgraceful. It's the behavior of godless slaves. I was particularly incensed when I read where Jews went to the Vatican petitioning for recognition. To have done so is to have committed treason against God and against Israel.

I've learned the hard way that Jews who prefer Pharaoh to God can't be reached.

What has been represented as Judaism by the Jewish clergy and the Jewish people has been the religion of a pacifist escapism, where acquiescence in the service of others' whims took precedence over the Law. When I think of a religious man, I think of Arjuna after his lesson.

One of the difficulties about being a desert refugee is that books that I want are sometimes hard to get. The desert has also stifled my winter pecan picking. It's the little things in my past weaving through me like an ancient web that have defined me but now no longer have too much immediate meaning.

I went back to my bunk to get into my suitcase and change shirts when I found my vile of sand that I packed out of sentiment.

When I was at the Chosen Reservoir in Korea, I was acquainted with a Jewish chaplain who was killed beside me one evening. After he died, I scooped up some of the blood stained sand that was under his body and have kept it to this day. I don't know why I brought it this far in life with me, except that I think he made me, at some level, feel like a Hebrew. I scattered the vile of sand upon the desert of his ancestors.

The camp has become an uncomfortable home. I find many of the people grounded in their own irrelevant cognitive addictions. The civility of the Jew is one of intensity and creation. It is a civility of intense imaginative thought. It has energized and challenged me in spite of my difficulties in adjusting to the immense escapism that comes with it.

A part of the blessing and the curse.

I remember the summer of 1947 that I spent in England outside of Birmingham with my father's first cousin Inga. She was one of the few Germans living in England at the time. She loved her heritage, and felt that it had been betrayed.

The mark of Germany, not to be absolved, is more the mark of Christianity (paganism) and of a failed Judaism (the slave's aspiritual escapism).

The Jews are the people of the Book that don't know the Book. They fail to see Life in the Book of Life.

Apocrypha: Ahikar 8.25

> *Young swallows fell out of their nest. A cat*
> *caught them and said. "If it were not for me,*
> *great evil would have befallen you." Said they,*
> *"is this why you put us in your mouth?"[22]*

It was as much the Nazi, as it was the average John Doe Christian partisan, for they are one and the same; both whelped by the same.

Instruments of unwritten church edict.

Christianity hides behind the Nazi to avoid blame.

When they cross themselves they pay homage not to love, but to a weapon of murder (a graven image) and to the freedom to murder.

This line remained hunters longer than the rest. Everything to them is a hunt; to them dying in the hunt is superior than relinquishing the hunt. Wars for them are for the sake of the hunt.

The antithesis of God is the human sacrifice.

Theirs is neither a heavenly seal nor an earthly seal but a dissent that through them has become an anti-Christ where their believers are the truer unbelievers.

I often use Jerzy Kosinki's *The Painted Bird* as bi-focals when looking at the European and his religious history.

The Jews who held the banners for Hasidism, Emancipationism, Europeanism, Communism, etc. etc., were too emaciated by false faiths to fight, except amongst themselves.

The Zionists were the only Jews not god-hunting, and it was they who survived.

The Jews of today believe that their holocaust occurred against them because they were Jews. This is false. The Jews were killed because they weren't Jews or anything.

Undefined.

The failure of Germany was that it had no Cicero or Brutus.

The failure of the Jews was that even if they would have had a Moses in the 1940's, he no doubt would have been ignored.

The price of veils.

As dusk approaches the speech of the sky tonight reminds me of an evening upon Lookout Mountain in Chattanooga that I spent with Harry Bubba Culver. We talked about the Civil War and how his great great grandfather was wounded at Shiloh while serving under General Forrest. The sky and the smell in the winds are the same now as they were that night with Harry. The

sky is the color of iris in bloom, and the winds tonight
seem to want to carry the world in its midst, not for the
purpose of design, but strictly for play.

I slept under a quilt I acquired from a fellow I worked
for one day helping him and his family get settled. It was
an old quilt but it was warm, and I thought the pattern
was unique, a menagerie of colored octagons. The
mothers in my tent used it during the day, and I eventually let them have it.

I went to sleep tonight with my thoughts lingering in
the glee of my past, and not on my disturbing thoughts
of politics.

I was told first thing this morning that a Sephardic
family in Betshan adopted me. I had heard something
about this Red Cross-like policy, but I'd never figured it
would reach me. The name of the family is Ben Sade, a
family of 22 including grandparents, and some extended
family. I am to have dinner with them Friday evening,
and I very much look forward to it. I will be face to face
with an unspoiled remnant of the East.

I arranged to get a ride on an army truck that brought
me about three miles from my destination. It was 2
hours before dusk, so I tried to take in as much as possible
on the way. Along the road I walked with an old Arab and
his mule.

I arrived at the Ben Sade house with some homemade
plum wine I managed to make in the camp last week. I
worked half a day in the mess hall for the plums, and got

a vat with an air lock from a soldier for a portion of the wine.

When I walked through the door, I was greeted by all the Ben Sades at once. They looked as though they were thrust into the 20th century from the deserts of long ago. I was wearing, along with my only tweed jacket, my Stetson and what's left of my brown work boots. This is now my Sabbath best.

The head of the household was Arich Abraham Ben Sade. He was about my age, a slender, and an observant man. His family practiced Judaism through the traditions of the East.

The Sabbath dinner was a warm affair that I enjoyed very much. This was the first home-cooked meal I'd had since I had arrived. Mr. Ben Sade spoke about his childhood in Fez, and I told him about mine in Robson.

These Eastern Jews are soft and delicate in their demeanor, much like the Thais. Their women are stunning. If I were a younger man, I'd marry one of these thoroughbreds in a minute. They're not only beautiful, but their God is my God.

I listened to one of the Ben Sades who had served in the war in Lebanon.

Had Abraham Lincoln been the president of Israel during this war, and Sherman his general, Beirut and Damascus would have endured the same fate as Atlanta; and the back of this Arab confederacy would have been broken.

William Tecumseh Sherman:

*We cannot change the hearts of these people of
the South, but we can make war so terrible
andmake them so sick of war that generations
will pass away before they again appeal to it.*[21]

It is the duty of those in the right to fully claim their
complete victory (ultimate victory).

For not to do so is sinful, and encourages the wrath of
heaven to side against you.

In discussion, Mr. Ben Sade asked me about my
religious past. I told him my mother's family were
Karaites and my father was a German of Lutheran
persuasion, but perhaps an atheist. My mother was
enamored by the occult, and she would read me
passages from the Kabbalah (odd for a Karaite) when I
was a child. I have been grounded in a perspective of
existence emanating from my parents that has made my
every moment a dilemma of faith.

I was glad to sleep in a home again, any home. In a
house so small, with so many, I was startled to be
given my own room. I tried to refuse, but it did me no
good. The space and privacy were nice, even if only for
the night. I will observe the Sabbath by resting and
enjoying the company of the family.

On Sunday I will go with young Eli to shear some sheep.
There's good money in sheep but there's more respect-
ability in cattle.

At 4:00 a.m. I heard young Eli come in my room to wake me. I was on the porch. Eli came out on the porch and looked a little startled. I said, "You're late — let's go to work."

Sheep are child's play when compared to cattle. There's not enough land over here to raise any cattle, but there soon will be. I enjoyed working the day with young Eli. I thanked him and the rest of the Ben Sades, then headed back to the tent city in the desert.

When I got back to the camp, there was a message on my bunk — Ilysa had died of a heart attack last night in Jerusalem. We never saw each other over here, and she was the closest thing to family I had. I sat down on my bunk and wrote Ilysa a letter.

My darling Ilysa,

The angels celebrated your birth because you were the Queen of the ballerina spirit. Your tender way could move me like God opened the ocean for our beloved. Whereforth will the poems of sweetness and compassion come unto me now that you are gone? Ilysa, my muse of the earth, you shall bring heaven forward.

I am your loving Karl,
By the light,

I gave this letter to a Mrs. Rothenberg, who was a lady in the next tent over. She came in and saw me writing and I explained to her that Ilysa had died the night before. She said she was going to Jerusalem in the morning, and she wanted to put my letter in the Wailing Wall, so I gave it to her.

I don't like the Wailing Wall. I don't like to wail about anything. Does not the Bhagavad-Gita say, "Do not lament."

The Jews have got to stop wailing and start winning.

I think the wall should be torn down. A monument to a defeated people is blasphemous. To me it states that their ideas were wrong because their morals were wrong, all of which went against God and the will of heaven. Instead of wailing about the outcome of their failures, the Jews should be pouring through their history to come to terms with those mistakes in their thinking that got them banished to the four corners. The banishment was a punishment, according to the book of Isaiah, and it has proven to have been an expensive punishment in Jewish blood. Until the third temple is built the Jews should replace the wall with a war college for any Jew who wanted to enter. This would be a place that would inspire the will, instead of submerging it into a meditative perspective of failure, as is the case today with this ridiculous wall.

After breakfast this morning, I saw a kitten that looked in need, so I dug through the garbage dumpster and found a carton of milk half full. I gave some to the kitten then took a sip myself.

I signed up for a work party that is going to build a new

settlement in the southern most part of the desert bordering Sinai. The place is so non-existent that it doesn't even have a name. I volunteered to go because I'm the most happy when working, and the conditions in the camp are becoming unbearable.

People know not the patience of the Creator.

On the truck, I sat across from a young Hasidic Jew. Looking at him, I think most men steeped in an observant applied methodology of ritual are trapped in their misunderstanding of God, not to mention his events.

Before I left Robson, I watched the film *The Paper Chase*. A line comes to mind as I gaze across the bus at this young chap dressed in black: *"It's hard being a living extension of tradition."* I'd say so because it's so hard for new ideas to enter, and by then it's usually too late.

The cultivation of individualism is the highest form of service, and anything less is a waste in nature that must be replenished.

The desert camp was barren. I saw a couple of army engineers setting up the base camp. The wind was blowing about 50 miles per hour, and I could barely see my hand in front of my face. I went into the cabin of the truck to get what little chewing tobacco I had left. By chance I glanced into the rear view mirror and saw myself. It was me all right, a little tanner, with a beard, and silver hair at my shoulders. My ascent into a Semitic mystic is beginning to show.

The winds of Thor are blowing tonight as they have all

day. Besides the difficulty of high winds, my first day here was pretty good. It was nice to have a tool belt around my waist again.

The young men from the diaspora don't know how to work with their hands, and I think they'll be slow to learn. They're not like their gung-ho Zionist predecessors who in the early part of the century worked so hard to meet their socialist ideal.

The men here with me now are possessed of a different spirit and nature. They are men educated in the arts of administration: lawyers, MBA's, and such. It's ironic to watch these high profile administrators, who so often accuse the rest of us as not being realist in their great civilizations, becoming lost and unadaptable to the changes in these civilizations when they find themselves void of a place and a role.

I acquired a transistor radio at the tent city, and have slowly begun to appreciate Arabic music. It's a far cry from Lester Flatt and Earl Scruggs, but I'm an evolving sculpture so what does it matter? My spirit shall stand in the Louvre someday and I shall be admonished there in invisibility.

Some of the men here are single, young, and hopeful frontiersmen who, like myself, wanted nothing more than to escape from the chaos in the tent city. I look forward to my days and nights here, where I hope to wander out into the desert alone with only God and my thoughts to accompany me.

I couldn't sleep so I got up and walked out into the song of the winds which has been blowing all day. I strolled off into the desert, not believing that I would come to this particular place at this time in my life. I lay down on the desert floor and fell asleep. I dreamt that I had once lived in this desert, as a banished scribe during a time of great tribulation. I wrote of the tribulation.

The modern world has entitled but not expressed them. I am forced to write them again.

There is little wood here, so the settlements are all pre-framed. All that is needed is a concrete based filler that takes a couple of days to set up. I think it's a novel idea.

I dug footings all day. I got word tonight that the tent city I just left came under sniper fire this afternoon. Those in the camp are still mulling around like they're in the suburbs.

The Jews of today must not fail to read the Christian and the Arab.

By the will of the anti-Jewish Koran and the anti-Jewish Christian clergy, both of which consider the Jews a cursed race, shall one come forth not only to prevent the sacrifice but to claim. He knows well of Israel's defeats that have come at the hands of those who fulfill the prayers of the cross and of the crescent.

The Constitution of His banner shall read:

To Complete

Islam is diligent in its pursuit to annihilate the state of Israel. If the Arab were the stronger, the bread ovens of Amman and Damascus would be used upon the Jews as weapons of genocide, and with the church's blessing. If the Jews fail to recognize these facts, the Jews could suffer a second Holocaust this century.

The Arab strategy is to bluff the Jews into a box, in which a war upon the Jews can be waged internally by hostile Arabs living inside Israel (a civil war), combined with a simultaneous external war waged by Arab states.

The Arabs cover their intentions by behaving as the weaker player.

Israel's embattled position with the Arabs embodies and personifies a future scenario for the people of the first world as it struggles to survive against the onslaught by the people of the third world and their ways.

Fifty years ago the Jews were thrown up in fire out of the belly of Europe as third worlders. The European Jews were a civilized, pacifist people, easily digested and easily thrown up. The third world peoples who inhabit the nations of the first world today do so deeply, with their cultures that are not easily digested.

These new guests that habitate the first world shall uproot, replace, and revolt, breaking down every host and those institutions that define the host.

For a moment I hear the "aum." I've just experienced the eternal now, a fleeting symphony whose march is infinitude. It is I that I hear within the still winds beyond thought and being.

I slept for a time, and was awakened by a terrible stench, and I seemed to be the only one to smell it. For a moment I felt that I had liver cancer, and that the terrible stench was coming from my liver. I awoke the fellow sleeping in the bunk beside me and asked him if he smelled anything foul. He said no. I told him that I did, and also that I felt for a moment that I had liver cancer. He said, "I have liver cancer." Then he rolled over and went back to sleep. When I awoke the next morning he was dead.

The forgone whispered before itself in tribute.

I posted a letter today in an old English mailbox. The English couldn't hold Israel, Egypt, or India, and today is losing its grip on Ireland. Soon the English will lose England to the darker ones from its previous colonies. Royalty in the House of England wavers before death.

At dinner tonight I spoke with Jacob Salta, a Jew from Rumania who came to Israel a year before I got here.

Salta said that he was wounded in the leg by a bullet in December of 1989.

He told me that he worked as an undertaker after the revolution in order to finish college.

I walked back to my tent and thought of the times that I had buried men or animals. When I did, I always saw the same vision: A pyramid of shallow blue light with the base standing upwards above the fully and freshly dug grave. The pyramid began to dissolve from the base downwards into the crown, using an overflow effect. Its pace was equal to that of a cat falling asleep in front of the fireplace.

Before I went to sleep, I thought back to the fall of the United States. Before it fell, I remember there were so many would-be-messiahs and so few men.

I worked with Salta today in the materials shed. He is a good worker and has more patience than I do. When I was young, I promised myself that when I got old, I wouldn't harp on the past. I didn't want to bore the young around me, and have them distance themselves from me. I am glad that I made that promise to myself. In watching Salta, I think the young are very much like opera: glee cast adrift into an island of playful intuition of the supersoul.

I lectured Salta in the shed today about bluegrass music, American Civil War history, and cattle ranching, among other things, as he lectured me on geology, East European history, and the polka. It's been a day of learning.

After dinner, I walked out into the desert like I've done every night since I've come here, just to be alone.

The encirclement around Israel has begun to solidify. The remnant of the Law awaits battle. Those that lead here lunge at their enemies with flowers. Television shall capture heaven's intervention.

With the exception of Salta, I've met few new friends here.

I'm going to go with Salta this weekend to Tel Aviv. He wants to go to the beach and meet some women, and I think that's what he needs. From Tel Aviv I plan to go on to the Golan Heights and spend the weekend.

From what I saw of Tel Aviv, it looked gauche. Everyone keeping up with the Jones'.

Once there was an Israel and a Judea; today there is a Tel Aviv and a Jerusalem.

When I was a small child, my father took me to Shiloh, Gettysburg, Vicksburg, and Chattanooga. He explained every battle to me in detail. I've acquired a book on the 1967 Six Day War, and shall read it on the Heights.

When I arrived at the base of the Heights, it began to snow. I closed my eyes and thought of my childhood and the times I camped out in the Smokies. Looking up at the sky, I got down on my knees and offered a prayer:

Oh, merciful father, do not let the flower throwers give away this stepping stone with a view that rises over the previous ones who bathe in milk below while they curse thee through us. Let the milk bathers bathe and frolic as I open the way unto you between the shameful flower throwers with wife. She is the virgin Dimona.

Isaiah 45:3

And I will give thee the treasures of darkness, and hidden riches of secret places, that thou mayest know that I am the Lord.

I sat up part of the night with a soldier watching the Syrian plateau. I asked him about a valley to the south that I had seen on his map. "Megiddo," he said. I thought Megiddo was folklore, but now that I've seen it, I realize that what my father had told me of it may not have been meant as folklore.

When I was a child, I was speaking with my father in his study and what was later to become my study. He was speaking to me about the First World War. It was the oddest discourse I had ever heard my father speak. He spoke of the dead men in front of him clamoring together in a circle, chanting in the language of the dead. They parted in their circle for the living men who were going forward, always forward. When a man of the living was killed, his corpse would become the holding place for snow, as his soul would join his brethren in the circle of the distant chant.

The morphine of the First World War met with the morphine of my father's cancer, so I left his study and left him in his difficult state.

An hour later, he called me back into the study, after he'd regained his senses. I knew that father was dying. I asked him what was the greatest battle in all history? He said, "Megiddo," then fell back again into a senseless state.

Early the next morning, I went to Megiddo.

With my first step into the valley came an enormous darkness, positioned about a centimeter off of my face and over my head.

As I kept walking deeper into the valley, the darkness kept growing until it looked as though I was a moving source to a huge river.

In leaving the valley, I feel certain that the battle for the Law will be waged here.

The future battle for the Law is the impetus for the Return, and for all returns.

I had never been to Jerusalem before, so I decided that I would stop and see it on the way back.

I was able to get a piece of bread and a cup of tea from an Arab food vendor, for a couple of hours work pushing tea.

On the way through Jerusalem I saw some Jews moving into east Jerusalem. The Arabs and the Christians were giving them fits. The Jewish star posted over their door was ripped off by a monk in protest. I bent over and picked up the star, and put it back over the door. I walked over to the monk and ripped off the silver cross that hung from around his neck. The monk walked away and I followed. It is a good thing he did, because I had my hand on my pistol under my overalls, and would have killed him, if he had added injury to insult.

Christianity attacks because it is false. Intolerant snake-oil salesmen. The Christian yearns to be regarded as the "new chosen" or even just regarded.

Adulterate.

Jews who longed to be Germans were guilty of the same.

One can learn from others, but cannot be others.

The day of the Chameleon is over.

I decided to stay in Jerusalem for the night.

The owner of a pool hall let me sleep on a mat in the back of the hall for helping him clean up.

While in Jerusalem, I kept thinking about the future battle for the Law. The acquisition of Job's faith and the appearance of Job's faith is not necessarily Job's faith. The acquisition of the Brahmin's way and the appearance of the Brahmin's way is not necessarily the Brahmin's way.

I visited the Temple Mount this morning. I am confident that the Ark of the Covenant rests beneath within the arterial network.

Having not yet retrieved the Mount, the Jews are saying to God:

> *O Lord, we are as yet still more fearful of men than of you, as we remain for the moment your unwilling covenant.*

I stumbled into a small obscure library and browsed for a bit.

I came upon a copy of Israel's 1948 declaration of Independence.

It stated:

> *The State of Israel will be open to the immigration of Jews from all countries of their disper-*

sion; will promote the development of the country for the benefit of its inhabitants; will be based on the principles of liberty, justice and peace conceived by the prophets of Israel; will uphold the full social and political equality of its citizens, without distinction of religion, race or sex; will guarantee freedom of religion, conscience and culture; will safeguard the Holy places of all religions; and will loyally uphold the principles of the United Nations.[23]

The State of Israel will be open to the immigration of Jews from all countries of their dispersion

O.K.

will promote the development of the country for the benefit of its inhabitants

False:
Tis for the benefit of God's will.

will be based on the principles of liberty, justice and peace conceived by the prophets of Israel;"

False:
To walk humbly in the light of God through the Law is all that was ever conceived of by the prophets of Israel.

*will uphold the full social and political equality
of its citizens, without distinction of religion,
race or sex;*

will uphold the full social.

Moral relativism.

and political equality

Only the humanist, socialist, materialist, liberals
and Baalist (both foreign and domestic) have political
equality.
The conservative, God-fearing Jews do not.

without distinction of <u>religion</u>, race or sex

False:
Treason against the God of Abraham, Isaac and Jacob.

*will guarantee freedom of <u>religion</u>, conscience
and culture;*

False:
Treason against the God of Abraham, Isaac and Jacob.
A continuation of the lunacy.

will safeguard the Holy places of all religions;

High treason against the God of Abraham, Isaac and
Jacob. The divine reason for the Jewish Holocaust.

and will loyally uphold the principles of the
United Nations.

They still bow down to men, even after the ovens.

Even in their Declaration of Independence they do not speak the truth.

Theirs is a Declaration of Dependence.

They are the Great Placaters.

On the way to the bus station, I walked through the hub of Jewish Hasidism, a neighborhood called Mea Shearim. A corridor of cultism.

I was glad to see Salta at the bus station. Seeing human activity again is reaffirming to me after this weekend where God used my mind as a playground for his worries.

We didn't arrive back at the camp until about 6:00 p.m., just in time for dinner. Salta met some gal in Tel Aviv and I'm happy for him.

Lying down to sleep I am unable to shake my experience at Megiddo.

As I fell asleep I began to dream that I was Michelangelo's God, with the outstretched hand. I was in an eagle's nest on an isolated cliff overlooking Jerusalem. Alligators were attacking the nest, and I was fighting them off with a spray bottle of fuel and a cigarette lighter.

I awoke the next morning, looked through the gape in my tent and saw the fuel area. I could have used some of that last night. I find it extraordinary that the alligators beat a path all the way to my door at the base of heaven. I pay tribute to their perseverance in hungry mindlessness. Then it dawned on me . . . the alligators had human eyes, they were human beings.

I spent the afternoon with an Irish priest named Donnigan whom I met at the first tent city. He is a very fine man with the voice of an angel. I made him sing me Irish ballads until I wept. I told him that soon the day will come when he will be asked to leave Israel. He said, "Yes. I know, but only so that we may all learn to become hosts in the manner of the Lord of Hosts."

For the next year I worked in the desert camp. As it grew it began to resemble a town on the Tex-Mex border, like maybe Laredo.

Salta was getting married in a couple of days, and I was to be his best man. I've already been to four weddings since arriving, and all have been men in my crew.

Salta's wedding was a pleasant affair. He asked me on his way out, with his new wife on his arm, "Do you have any advice for me?" I said, "Don't get too comfortable." We shook hands and parted ways.

General George S. Patton wrote in *War as I Knew It* the following concerning the Arab,

> *Another similarity between the Arab and the Mexican is the utter callousness with which both treat animals. Neither an Arab nor a Mexican would think of unpacking an animal during a prolonged halt. If the beast is chafed raw, the Arab does not even bother to treat the wound with*

*lard which is the invariable panacea with the
Mexican. He just lets it bleed and trusts to Allah.
Because a horse is dead lame is no reason for not
working him. All the animals are head-shy and
many are blind as a result of the cheerful custom
of beating them on the head with a stick. The
method of castrating sheep and cattle is unspeak-
ably cruel. I think that the reason that the horse
and donkey are not altered is due to their architec-
ture, which forbids the employment of the Arab
method. To me it seems certain that the fatalistic
teachings of Mohammed and the utter degradation
of women is the outstanding cause for the arrested
development of the Arab.*[24]

Genesis 11:12

*And thou shalt call his name Ishmael, because
the Lord hath heard thy affliction. And he
shall be a wild ass of a man: his hand shall be
against every man, and every man's hand
against him.*

In this age of thermonuclear weapons, the affliction is
spilling out upon the doorsteps of the many different
peoples who are contemplating with great focus upon the
spillage of the affliction.

The mass migration of the Jews from the West and
Russia may prove to be the foe that will banish the Arab

from Israel. The void left by the Arab enemy fills with Jewish enemies.

The Rabbis who are the wolves of weakness and have stolen their birthright from the priests (who themselves became corrupted), have corrupted this faith, while blaming the Gentile for our ashes. Two thousand years of Jewish capitulation in the diaspora must be credited to the Rabbis, since it was they who were responsible for guiding the spirits of the people. The flower throwers and their extended families of escapists also help to maintain the security of the veil.

Treatment of animals in the West is equally as barbaric as in the East. Western laboratories under the ideal of science or godless psychology apply with greatest zeal upon our fellow creatures all the indecencies that only a Joseph Mengele school of Naziism could inspire. Humanity is too lazy and too arrogant to look for other means to test. Humans must learn to treat all creation as they themselves would like to be treated.

The men of my crews have learned to work well with each other. We are producing very well, and I am pleased. Zvi, one of the coordinators here, asked me today if I would like to be a sheep herder. I was grateful for the opportunity and he knew it. He put his arm around me and said, "Go, go resolve."

I assumed my new duties this morning upon the plains of Judea on the anniversary of my parents' engagement. If I had a harp and a slingshot I could pass for King David.

Instead I have a walkman and a sawed-off shotgun that I brought over from Robson.

My first day on the job was quiet and peaceful.

It was nice to be away.

I walked through this desert mountain country all day without seeing a soul. I heard the Moslem call for prayer around noon, and figured the Bedouins around me were going to pray.

Islam was born out of Hagar's affliction.

Hagar could carry no faith for the most faithful of men.

Islam is a fanatic overreaction to faithlessness.

It has turned nations of men into fodder as proof of faithful behavior. Islam is angry, but peaceful when brother murders brother. The descendents of Abraham and Ishmael have replaced God with the anger of Mohammed.

The descendents of Abraham and Ishmael must rise above a thoughtlessness of Abraham and be thoughtful. I often hear the angry ones of Islam and the numerous ones of the cold peoples laughing against Israel in symphony.

I laugh at their laughter because I know the proposition for meekness that freezes the sun while possessing God's anger in duty.

The sun and I rose together this morning. I had a cup of coffee and a two-week-old jelly roll. I took a good look at my flock this morning. I had all black sheep. This was my flock all right.

I've still yet to shave or cut my hair in all the time I've
been here. When I'm in the settlement people avoid me,
except the men in my old crew who I see now and again.
The camp is now packed with new families from the
States, and I'm a stranger there now. I only go into the
Ag building for supplies at the first of the month, and the
rest of the time I'm out here.

I acquired a copy of *The Jewish War* and was struck by
what I read in the first few lines. Chapter I - Herod's
predecessors:

> *At the time when Antiocus Epiphanes was disputing
> the control of Palestine with Ptolemy VI, dissension
> broke out among the leading Jews who competed for
> supremacy because no prominent person could bear
> to be subject to his equals.*[25]

I now live like a Bedouin, and it's not a bad life.

I have met a Bedouin out here. He invited me into his
tent one evening for Turkish coffee.

I talked into the night with him and his sons. The Arabs
are ancient, like the Jews, but more charming and more
irrational.

I think that this desert will be an excellent place to exit
into the netherworld. I don't know what indiscretions
men commit in this life that the last thing they experience before dying is the feel of a bed pan and the smell of
detergents.

I met a kid the other day who was down my way and

who helped me watch the sheep. His name was Alex Torinoff, from St. Louis, age eight. He came over with all the other Jews from the diaspora during the peak of the exodus. He's here with his mother; his father is dead. Alex meets me late in the afternoons after school lets out. I think he's getting a better education from me anyhow. I'm master of the most important class and he knows it. Recess.

I met his mother, Polly, yesterday. When she looked at me her jaw nearly dropped to the floor. I guess I couldn't blame her. My hair is to the middle of my back and my beard is to the middle of my chest. I have an Arab sheath strapped to my stomach across my overalls, a sawed-off shotgun under one arm, with a Tennessee football cap on my head. If heaven's a formal affair, I know where I'll be spending eternity, not that it will matter in my case anyway.

Polly said that since Alex had met me he began to blossom a bit. She said she was happy we could become friends. After a while Polly would accompany Alex, and usually she would ask advice about this or that. One afternoon, she said, "Karl, this little country in a very short while is going to be in the eye of the storm. Why do you stay out here alone, detached from what is going on?" I said, "Polly, who's really detached and who isn't?"

In the period before the United States fell, there was rampant homelessness. I've been walking this desert for months now, and have never felt homeless once. Mindlessness was what made the streets of America rot.

I now call Alex, "Alex the Great." I've taken after my father by nicknaming everybody and everything.

I think I've acquired a bulldog pup for Alex. I told Polly, and she thought it wonderful. I told her I'd pick up the pup in a few weeks after it had been weaned.

The sheep didn't travel more than a hundred yards all day, and I don't think I moved more than a hundred inches.

Alex didn't come around today because he has the flu.

Mohammed and his Bedouins were passing through this month, and I told Mohammed that I'd like to travel with them. The Bedouins travelled all over Egypt, Jordan, and Israel, while no one seemed to care.

I made my arrangements for the sheep, and told Polly I'd be back, when I got back. I also gave her the name of the guy with the puppy. All I asked her is that she name him Winston after Churchhill, and she agreed. Churchill was a prophet of God as was Friedrich Nietzsche.

I met Mohammed at dawn at his camp.

It is a National Geographic-like experience travelling with the Bedouin.

I feel very comfortable and at home with the Bedouin.

The band was heading towards Jordan.

When we get to Jordan, I think I'll go it alone. I hope to walk from Jordan through Judea and Samaria into the other great tent city.

I had been on the road about two and a half weeks

before I found the spot where I wanted to get off. It was the Jordanian village of Husban about forty miles from the Allenby Bridge and Jericho. I began to walk down the road that leads toward Jericho. I walked for four days and didn't speak to a soul. Jordan from what I can see is just one vast Bedouin village. I have slept on the side of the road for four days, and tonight will be my last in Jordan. At 4:00 p.m. I finally crossed the Allenby Bridge into Jericho.

I was told by an Arab in the street where the Jewish tent city was.

I made my way up there by riding an Arab bus (one of the very last operating in Israel) up to Nablus.

What I saw was a retake of the first tent city I knew: one million Jewish men, women, and children, all in tents.

The hungry belly of the Ununited Nations rumbles.

Israel has gotten fat amongst those who are starved from their wealth and those who are starved from their poverty.

Many of the starved ones hunger for Jewish stew as a substitute for their own flavor.

The starved Ununited Nations will become a crafty hunter. It shall hunt Israel with a peacemaker.

The carnivore peacemaker will seduce by speaking of Jewish law, Christian love, Islamic charity, Taoist being, Confucian duty, Indian piety, and all others while claiming that he is but a humble being of truth.

He is in truth a being of untruth. He will appear as though a Brahmin, and many in Israel will rejoice.

They will rejoice as fools rejoice.

I rummaged through the masses of humanity here for a few days.

The last few weeks on the road I focused my thoughts upon the transcendental spirit of history. I try to see myself in it. I am a cell with eyes venturing towards the heart.

After spending ten days here I decided it was time to return to the desert and my sheep.

I boarded a cattle car at 4:00 a.m. heading south, and fell asleep. I dreamt I was making love with June under a waterfall. I awoke suddenly and pitifully unfulfilled. Had the trip been a few miles longer, I might have finished.

I checked in at the Ag center, picked up some supplies and then headed out. I left a note for Alex and Polly to let them know that I was back. It was a good feeling to settle back in with the sheep.

In walking today, I've taken notice of the rock formations and the vegetation here in the hills. This desert was under water at one time because there are sea shells in the hills. It's odd to think that I might have fished here once. I dare to think what I might have caught, maybe a camel fish or a sand crab.

My month away has made me appreciate the seclusion and solitude here. Tomorrow I'm going to keep my eyes open for a good grave site. I have a few possibilities, but what I'm looking for is a place in the shade where the wind blows. I want to succumb to the will of the earth with the same manners and grace as a grizzly chip.

I lay down on the desert floor and slept. I dreamt that there were two of me, facing each other in discussion. One looked like me now, while the other looked like me as a youth. In the discussion, the youth was the parent figure. I awoke early, disgruntled by this. I didn't like the feel of being scolded by a child. Yet the correctness of this child who I haven't known for so long is a living monument to my current distractions.

My messenger of death is my own innocence.

This ghost in the machine that is the machine will soon release, leaving what's left next to the shells in the hills.

A few days before I was wounded in Korea, I went to a little bar outside of Seoul. It was called Mama Sey's. It was filled with Korean women, closed in on all sides by purple curtains, and a white tiger that walked around the bar. Months later when I was at the VA hospital, my mind was cloudy and I didn't remember if I had dreamt it up or not. Years later when I returned to Korea, I went looking for the bar. I went to the place that I remembered, but I didn't see it. I walked around the block a few times, and all along asking people if they remembered such a place, but no one knew. Well, I figured it would be best just to let it go. I left and went on to the Buddhist monastery where I was to study for the next month. My last day at the monastery, I was coming out of the library and saw a doormat that was black with gold writing that said "Mama Sey's." I picked up the doormat and went into the old monk. I told him what I saw during the war, and then showed him the doormat. He said that Mama Sey was a Buddhist holy woman, and a close relation of the Dali Llama. The women surrounding her were her handmaidens. The white tiger you saw was the only one of its kind in the world. Her divine grace was visiting India, and the tiger walked over to her from out of the bush, submitting himself unto her as a protector; "What you saw was real;" he told me.

The reason I ventured out with the Bedouins and beyond was that I thought that out there in the wilderness, before the war for the Law erupts, I might come across another righteous one, like Mama Sey.

I feel relieved this morning. Alex showed up this afternoon and he brought Winston with him. As one joy maker passes another is born. If I had known that I would in some measure come to understand the meaning of my passing by drawing a relationship between myself and a bulldog, I would have celebrated years ago.

Alex will be out of school for a few days, so Polly said that Alex and Winston could stay out here with me for a couple of days. Alex was excited about staying out under the stars. I prepared mutton stew for Alex and myself; and for Winston I have dog food with mutton stew gravy. Most of the day Winston kept chasing the sheep, making Alex and me run after them. I taught Alex how to shoot my shotgun and pistol. He enjoyed being out of the camp and I couldn't blame him. We talked until about midnight, then the three of us dozed off. I awoke suddenly at about 3:00 a.m. when I heard a crash. Winston had gotten into the stew.

I took Alex and Winston back to Polly, and she was glad to have them back. Polly pulled me aside and told me that she would be moving to the tent city next to Hebron. She said that there was a man there for her and that she hoped they would make a go of it. She pulled Alex aside and told him of her plans. Alex began to cry, but I told him to act like a man and do his duty. I shook his hand firmly, looked him in the eye, then headed back to the desert.

Alex had to know unequivocally that the beautiful things of today must disappear for there to be beautiful things of tomorrow. I served my purpose by coming into young Alex's life, as he served his purpose by coming into mine.

I returned to the desert cheerful in spirit, but physically tired. Before I left Polly, I told her that war is on the horizon and to prepare herself. I was also glad that Alex had Winston. Winston was a rare find over here, and to Alex, Winston seems to be worth his weight in gold.

I arrived back at my tent in the desert just after dark. I sat on my blanket more depressed than at any other time since I've been here. I thought back on my life, and I think that an honest man has no place to hang his hat. He is important for the make up of the future, but is unwanted as a person in the present.

I walked with the sheep for a short while this morning, and decided upon the place that I would like to be buried. It is at the base of Mount Sinai beside a cave that I thought was rather peculiar. I found this cave while travelling with the Bedoins. The rock formations inside it were all foreign to the rest of the desert, and wrapped around and through each other, as though mixed in a blender. A cool draft always blew through the cave, right over the spot that I would like to be buried. I knew that I was dying and that the force of death within me was growing. I didn't know what I was dying of, but it didn't matter. All death is a solitary engagement — I'm just sorry that I will be escorted by sheep instead of people.

I returned to my tent and lay down, my body was hungry for sleep. When I awoke the next morning, I was blind. I fell into shock but must have come out of it. I never in my wildest dreams anticipated going blind. The first thing that came to mind was that I would be unable to read. Even in my last hours, I still hunger for poetry. I also will never again be able to earn a paycheck.

What must be overcome in the current thought process of the subconscious in much of humanity is the conviction of existence as temporal. This false view is the housing mechanism for thievery which is but the base man's response to the feeling of a grant of freedom before his execution. This subconscious conviction must be elevated to the truth that all existence regardless of temporal forms and identities is timeless. Men as individuals can elevate the subconscious conviction when they realize that their individual existence is but a celebration of the Law in individual form.

I ate some crackers, then drank a glass of water. I didn't know what time it was or even what day it was. I heard artillery fire in the distance. All I can do is sit quietly. I realize that my insignificance in this life that was so blessed by duration must have meant something to someone.

Upon the shores of death I feel joy and relief as I am Einstein's words;

To me it is enough to wonder at the secrets.

The greatest experience we can have is the mysterious.

I was sitting still listening to Arabic music on my Walkman, when I succumbed to the calling of death upon the dust of my ancestors.

The last spoken words of Karl Becker, as recorded by heaven:

"Retrieve the Ark."

Part III
The Hour

Like the Voyager penetrating into deep space do I fade.

* * * * *

One of the two letters left upon the body of Karl Becker.

Dear Alex,

I was grateful that the divinity in you mingled with the divinity in me.

By the light,

Karl

PS - Love to Polly and Winnie

* * * * *

A Black angel stood robed in white before my spirit. The angels holiness was great. Next to his holiness I gave way, as he possessed me. The angel spoke to me without words.

The many nations are virtues in perpetual conflict, all trying to be the will of God by themselves.

Many flutter unattached but unfree and in anger becoming vice, because they breathe by others' roots, as well as by the want of others' roots, often to gain in pursuits of foreign conquest, as they forsake themselves.

Many are lost in knowing and in not knowing.

The many tangled roots have wearied of entanglement and are falling away.

The Black White art of retribution proceeds by the will of the heavenly court.

Its judgement is rendered to be that

'The Hour of the Milk is No Longer White.'

'The Hour of the Milk is No Longer White.' is heaven's retribution against Europe that shall be submersion.

They are the closed ones whose identity shall be submerged.

They more than others have killed less for freedom than for rank.

A rank not bestowed upon them by heaven.

In so doing they have created themselves into non-definition akin to the darkness before Creation.

The cost of their order was too great to be sustained.

The freeing of the different strands shall require of the different strands a rekindling of lucidity away from within European brittleness that has been the dark side concerning their blessing of structure.

Heavens way is not revenge but to avenge.

Their hunt is over.

Does not a thing flow back into itself?

The power that destroyed Sodom and Gomorrah has been delivered from heaven to men so they may clean themselves from brittleness by a more severe brittleness that is without brittleness.

In so doing, God has set forth a resolve.

The afflicted twin must recant, or soon he too will be a sign.

There is no place for the manicured closed.

"Alex Torinoff was the home of the soul of your younger brother Maximillian Rudolf Becker"

* * * * *

The second letter left upon the body of Karl Becker:

All my life I have longed for this day.

I have prepared my body, my mind, and my spirit for the chance to stand before you now.

Yet, I will walk away from you if you hound me with your fears.

I am not Moses; I have no tolerance for your fears.

I will not be a burnt offering of weak and divisive men.

Hitler returned to you your identity but not your faith.

For even he couldn't do this.

Israel do not be blind. Rome's last gasp with its weapon of murder (the cross) shall be against you.

They believed that they could fool by hiding behind their false embrace.

Do they not lay in wait for themselves?

Crucifixon is what they have done and what they intend.

Murder is their god and their sustainer.

The music of the fluttering veil falling away from your eyes shall guide you against them.

You are no longer an unwanted houseguest.

If you choose to place a lesser one in my place, I will not remorse, because this is your way.

You are the pillars of my strength — do not have me sit amongst the dogs in the dust.

Recline not in your chairs before me.

Your lands and the soul of this nation is yet to be claimed by you.

Do not offend me by being squeamish and indecisive concerning your birthright.

You must be as the mulatto bastard who comes to know the strengths of the right and the left if you are to be the sturdy bridge, instead of the ravine of death that separates the two.

Israel is the sanctuary for the God of Abraham, Isaac, and Jacob alone.

Insult no longer our God by allowing in his sanctuary others' false gods to abide.

The God of Abraham, Isaac, and Jacob is a jealous God.

In the past you have shown disdain for the wrath of his jealousy by courting others' false gods into your sanctuary and calling it "humanity," while your survivors ponder the ovens and the ashes.

Do so no more.

Your bridge shall finally be the Law.

Israel, your destiny is to go alone.

Fear not the valley to the south that rumbles in the evenings, for it is only the pregnant mother of your remnant and mankind.

In the aftermath your hearts will be glad to look up into the dawn where you will see neither Mosque nor Church in your land.

The dust upon the Temple mount is open once again.

The next Temple you shall not fall out of grace with.

The next Temple shall be a coat of many colors that finally runs through your remnant as the harmony of the Law.

The Brahmin's reflections in the Ganges shall be seen here.

The Confucian scales of harmony shall find pleasure as the Temple's winds.

The Buddha's journey to end suffering will end here, while the silence of the Zen masters and the duties of their silence shall rest here.

Humanity shall cease in being a marketplace for the sale of souls.

And there shall soon come a day, after the battle for the Law when the child that leads them is them.

Heaven shall find rest from them in this day as the different free strands called by heaven "children" shall blow in the free winds of the Law.

Men will view men as tides, seasons, and cells, and without hubris.

And in this day humanity will cease in being the lemming.

FOOTNOTES

1   Russell, Kirk, <u>The Portable Conservative Reader</u> ; Penguin, 1982 New York, New York.

2   Strauss, Leo <u>On Tyranny</u> ; The Free Press 1991, New York, New York.

3   Shafritz, Jay M., <u>Words on War</u> ; Prentice Hall, 1990, New York, New York.

4   Weaver, Jefferson Hane, <u>The World of Physics</u> ; Simon and Schuster, 1987, New York, New York.

5   Yevtushenko, Yevgeny, <u>A Precocious Autobiography</u> ; E.P. Dutton and Co., 1964, U.S.A.

6   Haley, Alex, <u>The Autobiography of Malcolm X</u> ; Ballantine Books, 1983, New York, New York.

7   Schweitzer, Frederick M., <u>A History of the Jews Since the First Century, A.D.</u> ; Macmillan Co., 1971, New York, New York.

8   Hitler, Adolf, <u>Mein Kampf</u> ; Houghton Mifflin Co., 1971, Boston, Mass.

9   Packard, Vance, <u>The People Shapers</u> ; Little Brown and Co., 1977, Boston, Mass.

10   Ibid.

11   A letter from Voltaire to Frederick the Great, August, 1751, Edited by Burton, Steven, <u>The Macmillan Book of Proverbs, Maxims, and Famous Phrases</u> ; Macmillan, 1948, 1976, New York, New York.

12   Sharon, Ariel, <u>Warrior</u> ; Simon and Schuster, 1989, New York, New York.

13   Nietszche, Friedrich, <u>Thus Spoke Zarathustra</u> ; translated by Hollingdale, R.J., Penguin, 1961, 1969, New York, New York.

14   Whitney, Major General Courtney, <u>McArthur: His Rendezvous with History</u> ; Random House, 1955, New York, New York.

15   Durant, Will, <u>Our Oriental Heritage</u> ; Simon and Schuster, 1954, New York, New York.

16   Solzhenitsyn, Alexandr I., <u>The Gulag Archipelago</u> ; Perennial Library, 1973, New York, New York.

17   Shafritz, Jay M., <u>Words on War</u> ; Prentice Hall, 1990, New York, New York.

18   Edited by Baron, Joseph L., <u>Treasury of Jewish Quotations</u> ; Crown Publishers, 1956, New York, New York.

19   Churchill, Winston Spencer, <u>The Gathering Storm</u> ; Houghton Mifflin Co., 1948, Boston, Mass.

20   Barth, John, <u>The Floating Opera</u> ; Doubleday, 1967, New York, New York.

21   <u>The Memoirs of William Tecumseh Sherman</u>, The Library of America, 1990, New York, New York.

22   Edited by Baron, Joseph L., <u>Treasury of Jewish Quotations</u> ; Crown Publishers, 1956, New York, New York.

23   Laquer, Walter, Rubin, Barry, <u>The Israeli - Arab Reader</u> ; Penguin, 1984, New York, New York.

24   Patton, General George S., <u>War As I Knew It</u> ; Houghton Mifflin Co., 1947, Boston Mas.

25   Josephus, <u>The Jewish War</u> ; translated by Williams, G. A., Penguin, 1981, New York, New York.